LOVE OR MARRIAGE

When Hope rubs an old teapot, the last thing she expects is for a genie to appear. But Finn Masters is very real — and very attractive. Finn's financial problems and the old house he has inherited are none of Hope's business. She is already engaged to Todd and plans for the wedding are underway, so falling in love with Finn is not a good idea. Luckily, she still has one of her three wishes left.

Books by Fay Cunningham
in the Linford Romance Library:

SNOWBOUND
DECEPTION

FAY CUNNINGHAM

LOVE OR MARRIAGE

Complete and Unabridged

LINFORD
Leicester

First published in Great Britain in 2010

First Linford Edition
published 2011

British Library CIP Data

Cunningham, Fay.
   Love or marriage. - -
   (Linford romance library)
   1. Wishes- -Fiction. 2. Fiances- -Fiction.
   3. Love stories. 4. Large type books.
   I. Title II. Series
   823.9'2–dc22

   ISBN 978–1–4448–0919–0

Published by
F. A. Thorpe (Publishing)
Anstey, Leicestershire

Set by Words & Graphics Ltd.
Anstey, Leicestershire
Printed and bound in Great Britain by
T. J. International Ltd., Padstow, Cornwall

This book is printed on acid-free paper

1

Hope sat on the faded sofa in the panelled drawing room, clutching a cardboard box on her lap. The room was large and bright, sunlight streaming through glazed doors that opened on to a grass-tufted terrace. Once, the manor house must have been beautiful, but the old building had been allowed to drift into decay. Now the rooms had been stripped of their antiques, pictures taken down from the walls, and the china and glass auctioned off to the highest bidder.

She remembered the plans she had seen. Soon, the lovely old house would be nothing more than a pile of rubble.

Running her hand over the worn damask and chipped walnut of the little sofa, she wondered what had possessed her to buy something she had absolutely no way of getting home. She had also bought a box of miscellaneous china that was probably all worthless.

Admittedly, she had an empty house that was in need of furnishing — but a visit to a car boot sale would surely have made more sense than a day at a sale of antiques.

Bending down, she opened the lid of the cardboard box at her feet, hoping to see something of value, but the small china teapot sitting on top of several mismatched cups and saucers didn't do much to raise her hopes. She took the teapot out of the box and gave it a rub. It might be quite pretty after a good wash — and so might the odd cups and chipped saucers — but she still had to find some means of transport.

She jumped as a man sat down beside her. He had appeared out of thin air and, because the sofa was small, he was sitting very close to her. Uncomfortably close.

She tried to move away, but he turned to face her and she looked straight into a pair of intense blue eyes.

'I should stop rubbing that if I were you, in case another genie appears. One at a time is quite enough.'

Hope realised she had been absent-mindedly rubbing the teapot. She smiled self-consciously at him. 'The genie of the teapot? That's different. Do you grant wishes?'

'Of course.' He smiled back at her. 'But be careful what you wish for.'

As chat-up lines go, his were pretty good. She had a feeling she had seen him somewhere before, but that could just be wishful thinking. To go with the amazing eyes, he had untidy dark hair and a tan that must have come from foreign shores. The British summer hadn't been long enough or hot enough to produce that shade of deep gold. She noticed he already had the undivided attention of several women in the room.

Hope cleared her throat. 'For my first wish, I'd like some way to get my sofa home. They won't keep it here for me, and I came in a Mini.'

'No problem. I've been delivering

3

stuff for people all day.' He stood up and called to a couple of men in overalls standing by the door. 'They'll take your sofa outside to my van, and I'll carry the box for you.'

Thanking him, she followed them round to the front of the house where a number of cars and vans were being loaded with furniture and other items.

'Last journey today, Mr Masters?' one of the men asked, as her sofa was carefully loaded into the back of a white van. 'Most of the stuff is sold already, isn't it?'

'Most of it, but I'll be back in a little while to lock up.'

He wasn't just a delivery driver, then. She picked up the box. 'I'll take this in my car, shall I? I don't want to risk breaking the china.'

'Be careful with the teapot. It's the only home I've got at the moment.'

She laughed warmly. 'Thank you for doing this, Mr Masters. My house is only five minutes away.'

'The name is Finn. I'll wait while you

4

fetch your car, and then you can lead the way.'

Hope checked her rear view mirror several times in case Finn Masters decided to drive off with her purchases, but he stayed behind her all the way to her cottage. He was a very attractive man, and she had to remind herself several times that she was already taken.

Between them, they managed to get the sofa through her narrow doorway and into the house. The two downstairs rooms had already been knocked into one, the tiny kitchen was an extension built on the back, and luckily the front door led straight into the room with no hallway to negotiate. Finn Masters took most of the sofa's weight, and once they were safely inside, he sank down on the seat with a sigh of relief.

'Thank you so much,' Hope said. 'How much do I owe you?'

'Oh, a cup of tea will cover that — if you've got a kettle.'

'Of course I've got a kettle,' she told

him with a smile. 'I was just lacking a teapot.'

She filled the kettle and plugged it in, coming back to sit opposite him on a Regency dining chair she had bought on eBay. Most of the items in her cottage had been picked up at local auctions or house sales. It was amazing what people threw out.

'I only moved in two weeks ago and I don't have much furniture. Modern stuff just doesn't look right in here and antiques are expensive, so it's going to be a gradual process, but I'm getting there. My main priority was a bed.'

When he didn't answer immediately, she realised what she had said and flushed with embarrassment.

'Good choice,' he replied, his tone neutral. 'I think the kettle's boiling.'

She was glad to be able to turn her back on him and fiddle with the tea bags until her face cooled down. Still sure she had seen him before, she asked, 'Do you live locally?'

'I'm living in the old house until it's

sold. My grandmother left it to me, but it's turning out to be a bit of a white elephant what with inheritance tax and everything else. So the sooner I sell it, the better.'

So, yes — he definitely was more than just a removal man.

'The house is going to be pulled down,' she said. Of course, he must know that — but how could he allow that to happen, she wondered? 'Developers are going to build a load of modern houses on the land. I've seen the plans.'

'It's not definite yet. If I can sell the house privately, I will, but I may not have a choice, and the builders have made me a really good offer.'

He finished his tea and stood up before she had the chance to ask any more questions. 'I have to get back to the house and make sure it's clear of visitors before I lock up for the night.'

'Did you keep any of the original furniture?' Hope asked. She couldn't believe he had sold everything his grandmother had left behind.

'As much as I could afford. Like you, the need for a bed took priority, so I kept a nice Victorian brass bedstead for myself. I did buy a new mattress and bedding, I hasten to add.'

'This cottage is Victorian as well,' she told him, 'and I managed to get a cast-iron bed from a second-hand shop. It's only a copy, though.'

She couldn't believe she was talking about beds again. Whatever was the matter with her? She was practically a married woman, and Finn Masters was a complete stranger.

She thanked him as he climbed into his van and he smiled into her eyes.

'You still have two wishes left, remember.'

He hadn't asked for her name, which disappointed her for some reason, but her name and address would be on the receipt for the sofa if he should want to contact her.

Not that he would, of course.

She thought of ringing Todd to tell

him what she had bought at the sale, but he wanted her to let the cottage and expected her to buy hard-wearing modern pieces that would stand up to any damage inflicted by tenants. He had suggested she buy the house as an investment, but now she had actually moved in she loved the place, and knew she was going to hate having to leave.

She thought of the manor house and its spacious rooms. Pulling it down would be a tragedy, but planning permission would probably go through without a hitch because there was no dispute with local residents. As far as the villagers were concerned, expensive new houses would be nicer to look at than a Victorian eyesore, and the village shops could always do with a few more customers.

Today was Saturday, and before she met Todd she would have been getting ready to go out with her girlfriends. Todd didn't seem to mind if she went out without him, as he was often abroad on business at the weekend, but she felt uncomfortable when her friends started eyeing up men, or someone made a pass at her and she ended up having to explain that she was already engaged.

She glanced at the ring on her finger. The diamond was so big, most people thought it was a fake. She had been going out with Todd for five years before he proposed. She smiled to herself; it hadn't been the most romantic of occasions, but Todd wasn't a particularly romantic person. He had handed her the unwrapped box when they were having dinner at the Oxo Tower in London to celebrate her thirtieth birthday.

She had expected earrings or even an expensive watch, and when she saw the ring, she had been unsure how to react. Was it a dress ring? The stone looked far too big for an engagement ring, and she had never seen a diamond of that size — but he was looking at her expectantly, waiting for her to say something.

'Oh, Todd — it's really beautiful,' she

had said hesitantly, lifting the ring from its nest of ivory satin. Todd had reached across the table and took her hand, slipping the ring onto her wedding finger.

'It's about time we made it official, Hope. My mother tells me I'm not getting any younger, and neither are you, I suppose. If we want to have a family, we'll need to start soon.'

He ordered champagne, which cost nearly as much as her mortgage, while she sat looking at the ring. A family? That meant babies, and until then the thought of babies had been a distant dream. People had children later these days, and she hadn't realised there was any rush.

Even though the wedding wouldn't take place for nearly a year, Todd's mother had decided that late summer was the perfect time for a wedding and had already booked the Country Club for the reception.

Her workmates couldn't stop looking at the ring and asked her questions until her head swam — the main one being, 'Am I invited?'

She knew the answer to that, but she didn't want to hurt anyone's feelings. Although they were her colleagues and friends, she was almost certain they would be missing from the guest list unless she caused a fuss, and causing a fuss wasn't something Hope enjoyed doing. Most of her friends were Essex girls and enjoyed a good night out. Todd had been like that once, when she first started going out with him — but now he preferred the Country Club.

* * *

Finn Masters turned his car round and drove back to the manor in a thoughtful mood. He had seen Hope Brown briefly a few days before, when she had been standing only a few feet away from him, and for a moment back there he had thought she recognised him. But although she had looked at him curiously, it was obvious she couldn't quite place where she had seen him before. He wasn't surprised. A white coat was like a uniform. That was all anyone saw.

He let down the window of his rental car and wondered at the unexpected turns that life sometimes takes. If he hadn't received the letter from his grandmother's solicitors he might never have come home, and if he hadn't come home he would never have met Hope. And at the moment, he couldn't seem to get her out of his mind.

After working his way halfway round the world, the little village of Medbury was like an oasis to Finn. Sitting right on the Essex/Suffolk border, it was near several large towns, but when he drove through the main street he felt as if he had gone back in time.

The houses still clustered together round a small village green with the obligatory pond in the middle. A row of small shops catered for everyday needs and the local pub still looked just as inviting, with its hanging baskets and trestle tables grouped outside. The village hadn't changed all that much in the time he had been away.

Hope's cottage was tucked down a side street backing on to fields, and he was sure it would look wonderful once she had finished furnishing it with her second-hand period pieces. From what he had seen on his short visit, she had an eye for colour and a real flair for design.

He was sorry he couldn't do the same with the manor, just for his grandmother's sake, but the builders had made him an offer he couldn't refuse. Enough to pay off the astronomical inheritance tax and buy him a ticket back to Australia.

With his experience in Michelin star restaurants, the nearby Golf and Country Club had been only too pleased to offer him the vacant post of head chef, even if it was only on a temporary basis, and that was where he had first seen Hope. She had been having dinner with one of the local celebrities, a young entrepreneur, and it was then he had noticed the rock on her finger and felt a strange sense of disappointment.

When he saw her at the sale, he couldn't resist talking to her. Close to, she was even prettier than he'd remembered. With her amber eyes and hair the colour of a ripe chestnut, she was far too pretty to waste herself on Todd Bartlett. Finn had checked Bartlett out after seeing him with Hope at the Country Club, and found him lacking.

Todd made his money by skating very close to the edge on a number of deals, often covering himself by incriminating someone else, and Finn wondered if Hope really knew her fiancé. Had she been swept off her feet by the idea of marrying a millionaire? Or had Todd decided to add her to his list of conquests? She didn't appear the type of girl to be influenced by wealth, but looks could be deceptive.

With a sigh, he parked his car and let himself into the big, empty house. What Hope did with her life had absolutely nothing to do with him.

2

Sunday started out beautifully warm and sunny for late September. Hope had arranged to meet Todd for breakfast in the local coffee shop, which sold warm croissants with butter and jam and the best coffee in the neighbourhood, but she was running a bit late and hurried to get dressed, tying her hair in a ponytail because she didn't have time to mess with it. She quickly put on mascara and lipstick, the only real make-up necessities as far as she was concerned, and hurried out to her car.

When she reached the café, Todd was already sitting at their usual table, and she saw him look at his watch as she came in. She dropped into a seat opposite him and gave him a big smile. He didn't smile back. He looked as if he would rather be sleeping than eating breakfast; she reminded herself that he had only got back from Dubai the night before and was probably jetlagged. He was dressed in navy trousers and a cream silk shirt, casual wear for Todd, but he still looked as if he had just stepped out of the pages of a fashion magazine. She couldn't remember ever having seen him in jeans and trainers.

'You look tired,' she said sympathetically.

'Busy week.' He yawned. 'What have you been doing with yourself?'

'I bought a little sofa at the auction yesterday. It looks great in my living room — oh, and some bits of china.' She saw his brows come together in a frown, but tried another smile anyway. 'The sofa is really pretty, or it will be when I've re-covered it, and it needed a good home.'

Todd sighed resignedly. 'It's such a waste of money, Hope. I keep telling you to move in with me. My apartment is plenty big enough for both of us, and I already have all the furniture we need.

In a year's time we'll have a new house and your place will be full of students. Buying good furniture for it is totally pointless.'

'I still have to live there for ages yet, Todd, and I thought I might take some of my favourite pieces with me when we move into the new house.'

He laughed and reached across the table to take her hand. 'No, Hope, nothing second-hand from junk shops is going in our house. I want the best. I thought we could have an interior designer go through the place before we move in. You'll have enough to do with all the wedding plans, and a designer will save you having to worry about furniture and fittings.'

She pulled her hand back. 'But I want to choose the furniture we have in our home, Todd — not get someone else to choose for us. What if I hate it?'

'You won't hate it. An interior decorator will know what looks classy. Just think of those glossy magazines and the homes they feature. Real upper class. Our house might be in *Country Life* one day. I've already chosen the site, right on the edge of the estate and backing on to woodland. You'll love it. The builders have promised it will be ready in time, but if not, we can live in my penthouse until our house is finished.'

'Finn Masters might not sell to the builders. He's hoping that a private buyer might come forward.'

'Where did you hear that? That old house is practically falling down. No one is going to buy it unless Masters does it up, and a little bird told me he hasn't got the money to do that.' He patted her hand. 'Don't worry, my love. Finn Masters will sell to the builders, he can't afford to do anything else.'

'He's not exactly broke, though, is he?' Hope countered. 'The house must be worth quite a lot as it is.'

'The house as it stands is hardly worth anything — but the land is worth a lot to a developer.' Todd smiled at her. 'See? There's nothing to worry about.

Masters has got to sell to the builders. That's his only option.'

Hope knew pursing her lips would give her wrinkles round her mouth — her mother was always telling her so — but she couldn't help it. She pressed her lips together to straighten out the wrinkles and sighed.

'I suppose so. Anyway, let's enjoy our breakfast and then go for a walk in the sun. We mustn't waste a sunny Sunday morning. We don't get to be together so often now, do we?'

As they strolled through the park, she wondered why she felt so dissatisfied. She should be over the moon. She had a millionaire who wanted to marry her, a well-paid job, even though office work wasn't exactly what she had planned, and a house of her own — for the moment, anyway. Perhaps she would manage to find a tenant who would appreciate all the work she had done.

Todd looked at her. 'You're very quiet. What are you thinking about?'

'Nothing in particular,' she lied. 'Just

what a lovely day it is.'

'Perfect day for a wedding.' He squeezed her hand. 'Let's hope the day we've chosen will be just as perfect.'

His mother had chosen the date for the wedding. She had also chosen the table settings and the design for the invitations. Hope might get to choose her own dress and the dresses for the bridesmaids — if she was lucky — but there was already a problem over how many bridesmaids there were going to be, and she didn't really want a big wedding. The idea of wearing yards of white lace and filling a marquee with people she didn't know appalled her.

'Do we really have to go overboard on the wedding?' she asked Todd wistfully. 'I thought it might be nice to have a small ceremony, somewhere pretty — like a little chapel in the woods — followed by a wedding picnic for all our friends. It would save you a lot of money, too,' she added hopefully.

Todd snorted. 'You won't be able to sit on the grass in your wedding dress, and my mother's already chosen her outfit. You can't expect her to sit on a tree trunk in an expensive designer suit.' He rolled his eyes.

'Besides, I want to show you off. You'll look beautiful in a fairytale wedding dress with a bevy of beautiful bridesmaids. A big wedding and a romantic honeymoon, that's what I want.' He squeezed her hand again. 'You can decide where we go on honeymoon, as long as it's somewhere hot with a five-star hotel. I want you all to myself — for a week at least.'

Hope changed the subject. She didn't want to spoil the day by arguing.

* * *

They had a coffee at a pub by the river, and then Todd walked her home. He expected her to ask him in, but she knew he would scoff at her threadbare little sofa, so she told him she had some painting to do.

'I'm back at work tomorrow,' she

explained. 'So this is the only chance I'll get. Once the house is looking beautiful, I'll give you a tour.'

He laughed. 'Like, a tour of four rooms is going to take how long?' He gave her a quick kiss. 'Okay, I'll see you tomorrow evening. I might try and get a few hours' sleep while I can. I'm in this country for the next few weeks, so I'll be in the London office tomorrow if you need to contact me.'

Hope shut the front door and rested her back against it. What was the matter with her? Normally, she would have asked Todd in for a coffee and ignored his scathing remarks about her interior decorating. It hadn't bothered her before, so why now?

It was barely lunchtime, and she had the rest of the sunny Sunday to herself. Being on her own at the weekend was nothing unusual. Todd was a busy person, a workaholic who preferred to spend every day working on a new deal. Hope knew little about his job, only that he made a lot of money.

She knew he came from a very ordinary family. His father had run the local garage until he died from a heart attack. But the more money Todd made, the more he seemed to change. On the surface he was the same person. He did everything within his power to make her happy, buying her expensive presents whenever he went abroad on business and taking her to the best restaurants when he was at home, but they didn't laugh as much as they used to. Todd was often out of the country for long periods, or preoccupied with work when he was with her, and now they were engaged she was beginning to feel that she didn't really know him.

Too late now, she told herself. She had probably changed over the years rather more than Todd had done. He had always sought out ways to make money, and she had never questioned it. It just meant they could have more fun when they were together. Now his money seemed to come between them rather than making life happier.

Feeling restless, Hope carried her box of china into the kitchen and began to unpack the pieces. Most of them were dusty and needed to be washed, but she was worried about putting any of the delicate china in her dishwasher. Some of the old porcelain probably had a hand-painted design that wouldn't stand the dishwasher temperature. It would all need to be hand-washed in the sink.

She took all the pieces out of the cardboard box one by one and stood them on the draining board. She had the teapot, a little sugar bowl and two matching cups and saucers, four large plates in a willow pattern design, and two rather beautiful wine glasses that she decided would have to go on display. As she had paid only twenty pounds for the lot, she was quite pleased with herself.

Having washed everything as carefully as she could, she was about to pack the china back in the box when she saw an envelope lying at the bottom. The envelope was the same colour as the box, which was why she hadn't noticed it before, and it had a name written on the front in a flowing hand — *Finn Masters*.

Now what should she do? She couldn't open a letter that belonged to someone else, however curious she might be. The letter was intended for Finn — written by a woman, from the look of the handwriting, so probably his grandmother — but what on earth was it doing inside a box of old china?

The only way she was going to satisfy her curiosity was to deliver the letter herself.

Phoning first to find out if Finn was in would have been a good idea, but although she scoured the directory and even checked directory enquiries, there was no number for the Old Manor House. The phone, she was told, had been disconnected, so Finn was probably using his mobile phone while he was staying at the house.

She looked at her watch. It was one

o'clock, and only a short drive out to the house. She couldn't post the letter through his letterbox without telling him where she had found it, but if he was out, she could pop a note through his door asking him to ring her later.

She got in her car and drove slowly through the country lanes. Perhaps she should have waited until Monday and phoned the Country Club. Finn Masters was a very attractive man, but she was engaged to Todd and shouldn't even be thinking about another man, let alone going to visit him. For some reason, that made her smile. After all, there was nothing she could do about her thoughts, so she might as well enjoy them.

Driving past the village pub, she glanced at the tables outside in the sunshine. Sunday lunch, a very British pastime, was in full swing and all the tables were full. And — bingo! — at one of them sat Finn, reading a Sunday tabloid, a glass of ale in front of him.

Hope had left it too late to stop, so

she drove on up the winding road until she found a place to turn round. Knowing the car park would be full, she left her car in the shade of a tree and walked back to the pub, clutching the envelope in her hand.

He looked up in surprise as she slid shyly on to the bench opposite him.

'Hope?' His tone was questioning.

'I'm sorry,' she said quickly, 'I don't want to interrupt your lunch, but I was on my way to see you.' She held out the envelope. 'I found this in my box of china.'

He took the letter and looked at the front. 'It's my grandmother's handwriting. She wrote to me a lot when I first went abroad to work.' He turned it over and looked at the back. 'You found it with your china?'

'Yes. Your grandmother must have written it before she died and it was at the bottom of the box. But why not send it to you?'

He shook his head. 'I have no idea. I was moving around a lot at one time, so

28

perhaps she decided to hang on to it until I had a permanent address, or perhaps she just never got around to posting it. Maybe she left it in the house for me, and someone found it and put it in the box with the china. There were a lot of people in and out of the house after she died.'

He put the envelope down on the table between them. 'Will you stay and eat with me? I'm starving hungry and the food looks amazing, but I hate eating on my own.' He called over a waitress who had just appeared through the doorway. 'What do you want to drink, Hope?'

'Half a lager, please.' She could stay and have a drink with him; there was no harm in that.

The waitress took out a pad. 'Chicken, beef, or lamb?'

Hope looked at Finn helplessly. 'I can't — '

'Which do you prefer?'

'Well, chicken, but — '

'One chicken to go with my beef,' he

told the waitress before he turned his attention back to Hope. 'Oh, for goodness' sake, relax. You came to deliver a letter, your boyfriend can't kill you for that — and I'm not going to open the envelope until we've finished eating, so you might as well sit back and enjoy yourself.'

She laughed. 'You're a right bully when you get going, aren't you? Okay, I am quite hungry, now you mention it — but I insist on paying for myself.'

'News of my poverty has obviously gone before me,' Finn said wryly. 'I do have a job, in case you didn't know. I've been working at the Country Club since I got back to England.'

She clapped her hands together. That was where she'd seen him.

'The new head chef!' she said. 'They've been advertising their special gourmet menu everywhere.' She looked at him with new respect. 'I must say the food was out of this world. Where did you learn?'

He shrugged. 'All over the place.

Europe, to start with, but then I got the wanderlust and did a stint in Hawaii, and before my grandmother died I was working in Australia. I'm hoping the sale of the house will give me enough money to open my own restaurant somewhere.'

She raised her eyebrows. 'And here you are, eating at our village pub?'

'I appreciate simple food, and this pub has a good chef.'

Hope's roast chicken was delicious; it was pleasant to eat outside on the beautiful autumn day. A couple of ducks wandered over from the pond and she fed them bits of her bread roll. She'd never eaten at the pub before. Todd preferred to lunch at the Country Club, but he often got waylaid by business colleagues and left her alone, which she hated.

She found herself looking round anxiously once or twice in case anyone recognised her, and then realised how silly she was being. It wasn't as if she was cheating on Todd; she would tell him about her meeting with Finn next time she saw him. It was no secret liaison. Even so, she felt slightly guilty for enjoying herself so much. Finn had an endless string of stories about his travels abroad and his work in various top restaurants, but he also listened with interest to her plans for the cottage and the little garden at the back.

'You should have roses,' he told her. 'A cottage garden needs roses, and the old-fashioned sort smell wonderful. If you have room, you could have a little vegetable garden as well.'

'Are you going to open your letter?' she asked, when the waitress had removed their empty plates.

'I'd rather open it in private, if you don't mind. It's going to be quite difficult reading a letter from Grandma now she's gone.'

'Of course.' Hope reached across the table and impulsively put her hand over his. 'I was being really selfish, and terribly nosy.' Embarrassed, she took her hand away. 'Maybe one day you can tell me what she said.'

'Let me have your phone number, and I'll put it on my mobile. Can I ring you later, or will you be out with your boyfriend?'

'I'm not seeing him until tomorrow evening. He's sleeping off his jetlag at the moment and working in London all day tomorrow.'

'Obviously a very busy man.'

She thought she detected a hint of sarcasm in Finn's voice, but she wasn't sure. He wouldn't let her pay for her meal, so she thanked him and walked back up the lane to her car.

★   ★   ★

Once home, she changed into an old pair of jeans and a baggy T-shirt. Perhaps painting a wall would take her mind off Finn Masters.

Some time ago she'd bought a white bedspread dotted with tiny pink rose-buds, which meant she was rather limited with her choice of wall colour in the bedroom: It had to be pink, and the shade she'd chosen was perfect. Not too bright, just a flush of pale rose. Surely Todd couldn't object to that?

She finished one wall and stood back to admire the effect. It would dry a shade lighter, and then the colour would match the bedspread perfectly.

By the time she finished the second wall, the sun had moved and deep shadows filled the room. She looked at her watch, surprised to see it was nearly seven o'clock — and at that moment the phone rang downstairs.

3

Finn smiled when he heard her voice. She sounded breathless and slightly husky. Very sexy.

'Hi,' he said. I've read the letter — and as you have part ownership, I think you should see it. Do you feel like a drive over here? I can give you a tour of the house as well, if you like. You might not get another chance to look round before it's pulled down.'

He heard her draw in a deep breath. 'I don't know. I've been painting the bedroom and I'm covered in paint at the moment.'

'Come as you are. No one is going to see you, except me.'

'Can't you just tell me what's in the letter?'

'No, you need to see it. I'll be looking out for you.' He smiled as he put the phone down. For some reason their conversation always seemed to have something to do with the bedroom. Why was that, he wondered?

By the time she arrived at the manor it was almost dark. He met her at the front door and she followed him into the hall. Now empty, it seemed a lot bigger, and he saw her glance up at the naked bulb hanging from the ceiling. It did its best, but still left most of the large space in shadow.

'The rooms are too big to light with just one bulb. There used to be a chandelier in here, a really old one, converted to electricity, but that was one of the first things to be sold. I would have kept it, but I got offered a ridiculously good price.'

He led the way into the kitchen where a silk-shaded table lamp standing on the dresser added extra light to the room. He'd moved the kitchen table to the middle of the tiled floor, and put a wooden chair on either side.

'I kept the dresser,' he told her, 'even though I could have done with the money, and a few other bits and pieces like the table and chairs. I still need somewhere to sit and eat.'

He watched her look round the room, assessing its potential. If she lived here, she would soon have it back to its original state — no doubt with the Aga up and running, and copper pans hanging from the ceiling. Hope Brown would be good for a house like this. He remembered his grandmother teaching him to bake in this room. He had loved cooking, even then.

'I've already ordered pizza,' he told her. 'It should be here any minute, and I've got a bottle of wine — but you only get one glass because you're driving home.'

'You didn't say anything about food.' She frowned, and he thought he was about to frighten her away.

'You don't have to eat if you don't want to.' He shrugged, hoping she'd think he didn't care either way. 'I'm just saying there will be plenty if you're feeling hungry again. It's been a long time since lunch, and I thought you might fancy a snack. I ordered pepperoni with mushrooms and onions, and a margarita with olives and anchovies. I thought you'd like one or the other.'

He was grateful for a thumping on the front door that made her reply unnecessary. She followed him out to the hall, and he saw her smile when the pizza delivery boy thrust two boxes hastily into his hands and ran back to his bike.

Finn laughed. 'Good job I paid by card over the phone. He'd never have waited for his money.'

'He must believe the stories about this place. The local kids were a bit scared of your grandmother.'

'I know. They thought she was a witch. I think she went a bit strange in her later years. I should have come back sooner.'

Finn opened the fridge and took out a tub of coleslaw. The pizzas were still steaming, already cut into wedges. He handed Hope a square of kitchen roll and a teaspoon, hoping the smell of the food would convince her to stay.

'Fingers for the pizza, spoon for the coleslaw, and kitchen roll to wipe the goo off your face,' he joked. 'Okay?'

She helped herself to a slice of the anchovy pizza. 'Do I get a glass for my wine, or do we drink out of the bottle?'

He tossed her a plastic beaker from a pack. 'Will a paper cup do?'

'Goodness,' she said with a smile. 'You certainly know how to give a girl a good time.'

'Nothing but the best.' He smiled back at her across the table. 'Are you having a good time?'

She ignored the question. 'Thank you for the food. That's twice you've fed me today. For a little while, you made me forget all about weddings and marquees and mothers-in-law. The wedding isn't for nearly a year yet, but I'm feeling frazzled already.'

They finished the food. Finn collected the empty pizza boxes and tossed them into an old metal bucket he was using as a waste bin.

'For someone who wasn't hungry, you did a great job.'

'I didn't say I wasn't hungry.' She rolled her makeshift napkin into a ball and lobbed it into the bucket. 'Thank you again. That was lovely. One of the best meals I've had for ages — and I'm not being sarcastic. I have trouble with posh restaurants. The portions are so small, you need at least four courses to avoid starvation and I'm always afraid I'll use the wrong knife.'

'It's possible to manage most food with just your fingers, I learned that in India, and chips are specially made for dunking in tomato sauce. I've worked in some of the best restaurants in the world, and food can be incredibly pretentious at times.'

Standing up, he took the crumpled envelope from the dresser and handed it to her. 'You've been very good, not asking about the letter.'

'I thought you'd get around to it in

the end. After all, that was why you asked me here, wasn't it?'

He smiled to himself. That was only one of the reasons. 'Read the letter, Hope. I'm in a bit of a quandary.'

She took the folded paper out of the envelope, glancing at him worriedly, and he saw her eyes go to the date. The letter was dated two years ago, well before his grandmother died.

He moved closer to Hope and read the letter again over her shoulder.

⋆ ⋆ ⋆

My dear Finn,

I am leaving the house to you because you are the only family I have left. I know you loved this house when you were a little boy, and I hope that one day your own children will fill the house with laughter again. I only wish you could have stayed with me a while longer before your mother took you away. I so enjoyed looking after you.

With all my love.

* ★ *

The letter was signed in his grandmother's flowing handwriting. It was, indeed, a letter from the grave.

'You can't sell the house,' Hope said softly, and when she looked up at him, he saw tears in her eyes.

'I don't know what else I can do. The bank won't give me a loan. In its present state the house could take years to sell, the bank knows that, and I don't have enough money to renovate it.' He squared his shoulders and took a breath. 'Are you ready for the grand tour?'

She nodded mutely and he desperately wanted to take her hand, touched that she cared about his grandmother, even though she had never met the old lady. He wished with all his heart that he could keep the house — but time was running out.

They started on the ground floor. The hall was tiled in a traditional pattern common in Victorian houses, and there was a laundry room beyond the kitchen, the floors still flagged in their original terracotta tiles. The main rooms all had heavy oak planks on the floor; he still remembered being told not to run because it made too much noise. A room off the hall had been a library, with walls of empty shelves once filled with books. He had been disappointed, as a little boy, to find that none of the books had pictures.

Hope turned in a slow circle. 'There should be a button-back Chesterfield,' she said, 'and a desk with a leather blotter and a china inkwell.' She looked at him with shining amber eyes. 'Did you ever play hide and seek in this house, Finn? Did your grandmother let you have friends round? She must have done. It would have been lonely here on your own.'

When he didn't answer she turned. Their eyes met, and he knew she must have caught the flicker of sadness in his before he looked away.

'My grandmother gave birth to two

children,' he said. 'My mother had a twin sister, but she didn't survive. My grandfather died when my mother was in her teens, and then my mother got married and moved away, leaving my grandmother on her own.

'When I was born, it cramped my mother's style. I don't know whether I was planned, or whether I was just an accident. My mother liked to travel with my father and it would have been difficult with a baby, so she left me with Grandma until I was six years old. I had just started going to the local school and I liked it there, but by then my mother and father had decided that now I was older, they could take me with them.'

'So your grandmother was left on her own again.'

'To be honest, Hope, I didn't even think about it. Looking back, I was thoroughly selfish. Grandma wouldn't leave this house, even though it would have been sensible to find something smaller. She was the last of the

Hamiltons, the last of the family line; she refused to sell the family home.'

'Didn't your mother visit her?'

'My mother and father were abroad most of the time. Dad died of a heart attack when I was in my teens and then my mother was killed in a car crash. I think Grandma went a bit strange after that.'

'It must be really sad to outlive your children,' Hope murmured. 'And you must have missed your parents terribly.'

Hope was a sympathetic listener, and he had told her more about his family than he had ever told anyone. He moved away from her and started up the stairs, telling her to be careful. Oak panelling and wood banister rails made the staircase dark, and he hadn't bothered to put a light on the landing above. Worried that Hope might find the dim light daunting, Finn opened the first door they came to and flicked a switch. Again, there was just a bulb hanging from an ornate ceiling rose.

This room had panelled cupboards flanking one wall, the doors half open, the interiors empty.

'This house is early Victorian,' Hope said. 'So there was more than one generation living here before your grandma and grandad moved in. Can you imagine what the clothes hanging inside these wardrobes would have looked like then? Gowns in satin and silk, and dresses for afternoon tea on the lawn. That was the time of a tiny waist and a full skirt, before the bustle became fashionable. The shoes would be arranged in neat rows, with hats on the shelves above. I know there was a lot of poverty, but wouldn't it have been wonderful to be a part of the gentry in those times?'

He couldn't help smiling at her enthusiasm. 'I bet a wedding dress from that period would have been a tad uncomfortable, though.'

'Goodness, yes.' She shuddered. 'I would have had to wear a corset.'

Further along the landing Finn

showed her the room he had occupied as a child, a frieze of zoo animals still visible under the picture rail. The first time he had walked into this room after coming back to the house, he had been able to remember every detail — even the names he had chosen for the animals. He opened another door to show Hope what had once been the equivalent of an en-suite. His very own bathroom. A tiny room that now held only a grimy washbasin, an enamelled bath, and a toilet with a broken wooden seat.

'This was my room when I was a child. I had almost forgotten the animal frieze. I used to talk to the animals when I was trying to go to sleep.'

'Did they talk back?' Hope asked him with a smile. 'And did you have hot water in your bathroom? I have a vision of a maid filling your bath with water from a jug.'

'No maid, I'm sorry to say. There's a boiler in an outhouse out the back. Grandfather wouldn't have it in the cellar because that was where he kept his wine.'

This was a house where money had eased the lives of the occupants, unlike the folk in the village who would have had to manage without the advantages of indoor plumbing. There was still an old pump in the centre of the village green.

His grandparent's room had an amazing view of the gardens and the adjoining woodland. Hope pressed her nose against the glass.

'Where does the boundary end, do you know?' she asked him. 'I don't wonder that someone wants to buy all this, it's beautiful.'

He crossed the room to stand beside her. 'It's not that big, actually. There's only just over two acres, all told — not a lot for a manor house. The boundary ends at the stream on one side and just in front of the trees on the other. The builders want to rip up most of the trees and cram as many houses onto the plot as they can. I had a look at the preliminary plans.

'One or two houses would be okay, I suppose, but that's not what the builders want. Particularly not this lot of builders. They have a reputation for staying just within the legal limit for safety, and I hate to see unnecessary, ill-thought-out building schemes ruining the countryside.' He sighed.

'This house has been sitting here for over two hundred years. It deserves a little tender loving care, not a demolition order.' He walked to the door, waiting for her to catch up. 'Come on, there's still a lot to see.'

The house, even in its present state, was quite impressive. The main bathroom was enormous. Sitting high on clawed feet, a steel bath straddled a corner, still looking quite grand in spite of a few rust spots. A pipe rose from the floor and curved over the end of the bath, ending in what must once have been a state-of-the-art tap arrangement. The washbasin and toilet were both made of china dotted with little blue flowers.

'Wouldn't it be wonderful to restore all this to its former glory?' Hope mused. 'I'd get a landscape gardener to find the old plans and put the garden back to how it was, and rebuild the wall round the boundary so the local kids can't get in and pick the flowers.' She looked down. 'And just think what these planks would look like, sanded and polished. I could spend hours looking for the right rugs. What a pity the furniture had to be sold.'

'You have the little sofa,' he said with a smile. 'You saved that.'

She smiled back. 'Yes, I did, didn't I?'

'I'll show you the cellar. When my grandfather was alive, no one was allowed in the cellar but him. I don't think Grandma knew he kept his wine down there.'

Finn turned off the lights as they left the room, plunging the landing into semi-darkness. He went down the stairs first so Hope could follow, but the stairs were chipped in places and she caught her foot on one of the treads, pitching forward before she could stop herself. He heard her give a little squeak of fright and turned round on the stair below, feeling his heart stop for a moment as she toppled towards him. He managed to catch hold of her with one arm, clamping his other hand to the rail. She fell heavily against him, and for a moment he thought they were both going to plummet to the bottom of the stairs, but he steadied himself and managed to keep his feet.

Thoroughly shaken, he held her close against him while he caught his breath. He couldn't bear to think what would have happened if he hadn't been there to catch her. It was a long way down.

After a moment, he sat down on the stair, helping her sit beside him.

'Rest up for a minute,' he said, trying to keep his voice steady. 'You nearly had me down the stairs as well.'

'I'm sorry,' she said shakily. 'I caught my foot. Thanks for catching me.'

'Any time,' he answered.

She stared at him seriously for a minute, and then she giggled. 'You must admit it was quite funny.'

'It wouldn't have been funny if we'd both gone tumbling down to the bottom. There'd have been lots of broken bones, and I haven't got my mobile phone handy to call for an ambulance.'

'Mine's in my bag,' she said, stifling another giggle. 'But I wouldn't have been able to get to it, would I? Not if I had lots of broken bones.'

'So we'd be lying together at the bottom of the stairs until someone came and found us.'

'Or poured the foundations for the new houses on top of us, and then you'd never be able to get back into your teapot.'

He turned to look at her. 'That wouldn't upset me too much.'

Her face was indistinct in the gloom of the dark stairwell, but as he looked into her eyes, he forgot all his good intentions. She could have moved away

— he gave her plenty of time to do so — but instead she met him halfway and her sweet mouth responded eagerly to the touch of his own.

Afterwards, he put the kiss down to the shock of seeing her fall towards him, but he knew he was kidding himself. He had wanted to kiss her from the moment he first saw her at the Country Club. It was as if everything that had passed between them had been leading up to this moment. His grandmother's letter had linked them together as surely as if she had been orchestrating their movements.

Hope scrambled to her feet but he caught her hand. 'Wait. You might fall again. Let me go ahead.'

When they reached the bottom of the stairs she headed for the front door. 'It's late. I have to go.'

He helped her pull open the heavy door. 'We'll save our expedition to the cellar for next time, then.'

'That might not be a good idea.' She stared at the floor so she wouldn't have to look at him. 'You know I'm engaged to Todd Bartlett.'

'Then he should have been here with you tonight. I wouldn't have let you drive out here in the dark — not on your own.'

She started towards her car, but turned. This time she did look at him.

'You can't sell this house, Finn. It's part of your history.'

4

The drive home was uneventful. Hope spent the whole journey trying to work out what she was going to say to Todd. Why had she gone to the house to see Finn? If she didn't know why herself, then there was no way she could explain her visit to Todd. She shouldn't have allowed another man to kiss her when she was already engaged — and she certainly shouldn't have enjoyed the experience.

She could blame her indiscretion on the fact that she had nearly broken her neck falling down a flight of stairs, but that wasn't strictly true. She hadn't just allowed Finn kiss her, that would have been bad enough, but she had kissed him back — which might suggest that there was something seriously wrong with her present relationship.

Pulling up at her house, she wondered if that was what she should tell Todd — or if, indeed, she should tell him anything about the incident at all. If being honest was just going to upset him, perhaps it was best to keep quiet. After all, she had done nothing to be ashamed of, she told herself defiantly.

The red light was flashing on her answering machine. A message from Todd asking her where she was, and to call him back when she got in. She deleted the message. She still hadn't made up her mind what to say to him.

By the time she was ready for bed, she had come to a decision. She had been going out with Todd for a long time. Now they were getting married, just as everyone had expected, and trying to rock a relatively steady boat was stupid. She wouldn't see Finn any more, because it would cause too many problems. One man at a time was quite enough.

Falling asleep almost immediately, she dreamed of playing hide-and-seek in the old house — but then Todd was chasing her down a dark hallway and she couldn't find Finn. She could hear him calling to her but all the doors were locked, and she had to get to him before the bell stopped ringing . . .

She woke with a start and slapped her hand on her alarm clock. It took her a minute to work out what day of the week it was, but she eventually decided today was Monday, and she had to go to work.

After a quick shower in her newly installed bathroom she ate a bowl of cereal and thought how nice it was to have a whole house to herself. Once she got past twenty-five, living with her mother had not really worked.

She frowned at her reflection in the mirror. Her hair had been shaped and cut by her mother's hairdresser, a sweet young man who tutted and fussed and suggested she had red highlights, something she had somehow found the strength to refuse — and her clothes were the same day after day, a smart suit or skirt and a blouse that didn't show any cleavage. The office uniform. Heels were optional, so she usually settled for flat pumps rather than totter about all day on stilettos like the other girls.

With a sudden surge of rebellion, she took off her sensible navy skirt and white blouse and started all over again, choosing a brightly coloured cotton dress and a pair of sandals that showed off her painted toenails. She tied her hair back in a cool ponytail and made her way to the council offices where she worked, feeling absolutely great.

She was starting to regret her bravado by the time she slipped into her workstation, very conscious that none of the men were looking at her face. Perhaps the halter neckline was a little low. Her supervisor, a woman who insisted on being called Mrs Potter, even though everyone else used first names, came over to have a word.

'You look very cool and summery, Hope, but perhaps a little too casual for the workplace. We have an important politician coming to see us this afternoon, so it might be a good idea to go home in your lunch break and change. A tailored suit looks so much more businesslike.'

Hope felt like telling Mrs Potter what she could do with her tailored suit on a sunny day, but she needed the money in her bank account every month, so she nodded her head contritely. She felt like going home at lunchtime and not coming back.

She was nearly halfway through the pile of work on her desk, when her phone rang.

'I'm taking you to lunch,' Todd said, and hung up before she had a chance to so much as reply.

It was bad enough getting bossed about at work without getting orders from Todd as well! She knew what time he would pick her up without asking; he was a creature of habit and expected her to be waiting for him when he arrived.

'You look very summery,' he said, as he held open the door of his BMW.

Hope was beginning to think 'summery' must be a euphemism for something entirely different.

'Can we go somewhere else today?' she asked. 'It's such a nice day, I don't fancy the Country Club. Can we eat in that little bistro by the river?'

She was keeping her fingers crossed under the seat. He had to agree. She couldn't bear the thought of coming face to face with Finn.

'Where were you last night?' he said as if she had not spoken. 'You didn't answer my phone call.'

She attempted a puzzled look. 'What time did you ring me, Todd? I was so tired after painting the bedroom walls, I went to bed early.'

'Never mind. It really doesn't matter.' Completely ignoring her request, he drove straight to the Country Club. 'We can eat outside on the terrace if you like, but you'll probably get bugs in your food.'

Finn wasn't likely to leave his kitchen to come out on to the terrace, but she still felt twitchy. She kept telling herself she hadn't actually cheated on Todd, it had just been a spur-of-the-moment kiss, but she still felt guilty.

'You said you know the chap who owns the Old Manor House; met him at the auction or something.' Todd waited while the waiter took their order and Hope's heart thudded. 'I want you to do something for me, Hope. A bit of undercover work.'

She started to say something, but he held up his hand.

'Hear me out, Hope. You seemed to think there was a chance this Masters person might not sell, and I've spoken to my colleagues about this. They stand to lose a lot of money if the land doesn't become available.'

'How? I don't understand.'

Todd patted her hand. 'You don't need to understand. I just want you to find an excuse to contact Masters and find out what the situation is. He's up to his eyes in debt, so he's got to sell to someone, but we need to know if he's had another offer. Remember, Hope, if the builders don't get the land to build on, you don't get your new house.'

Hope stared at him in open disbelief. 'You're wanting me to spy for you?'

'Don't be ridiculous, I'm not suggesting spying on anyone, but you've already met the man once. Just be friendly.'

Hope felt slightly sick. 'How friendly?'

'For goodness' sake, Hope.' Todd unrolled his napkin. 'You make it sound as if I'm asking you to do something improper.'

She got to her feet. 'Aren't you? I think you just asked me to chat up another man for your own personal gain. In my book, that's called pimping.'

She got to halfway to the door before he caught hold of her arm and swung her round roughly to face him.

'Come and sit down, and stop behaving like a child. I won't let you walk out on me — not here.'

She wrenched her arm away. 'Just watch me.'

She made it all the way to the car park before she cried. Not loudly or obviously, just a quiet sniffle — mainly because she had no way of getting home. If she'd had a set of keys for Todd's BMW she would have taken it, even though he had never let her behind the wheel.

Suddenly she saw Finn walking towards her, and hastily wiped a hand across her face.

'Lovers' tiff?' he asked gently.

She shook her head. 'Not really. More than that, I think.' She gave him a wobbly smile. 'I'd made up my mind not to see you again.'

'And here I am. We genies pop up all over the place like the proverbial bad penny. Can't get rid of us, however much you try.'

'Can I have my second wish, please? I need a taxi to take me home.'

'Won't he come looking for you in a minute?'

She shook her head. 'No. I humiliated him in front of people he knows by walking out on him. He'll send me to Coventry for a week and then pretend it never happened.'

Finn took a mobile phone from the pocket of his white coat. 'You're worth more than that, Hope.'

She waited while he called for a taxi to pick her up. 'I know.'

He stayed with her for the few minutes the taxi took to arrive and insisted on paying in advance. 'I'll call you,' he said.

'Like I said before, probably not a good idea.'

He just smiled. 'I can't compete with Todd Bartlett, Hope, you know that. It just depends what you want out of life.'

* * *

Finn watched the taxi drive away, wondering what the argument had been about. None of his business, of course, but highly intriguing. He stuck his head into the restaurant to see Todd Bartlett had moved to a table with three other men. They were laughing quite loudly, and Finn sighed. It was a good thing he wasn't the kind of chef to spit on the food.

He knew he had to step back and let her sort her life out. He wouldn't make a move again until she told him she was free, but he didn't really expect that to happen. She was engaged to a million-aire and hardly likely to give up all that for a penniless chef, even if he was one of the best in the country — maybe even the world. He smiled to himself. No way to test that out, really, but it sounded good.

Hope had told him not to sell the house, and he was going to do as he was told. How, he had no idea, but something would turn up. Until then, he would start renovating. Paint didn't cost that much and he already had a mop and bucket. He did shift work at the Country Club, so he had a couple of afternoons free each week, which was just as well. Slapping paint about in the dark would not be a good idea. Once the place was clean and freshly painted, he thought he would start on the garden.

Feeling much better, he went back into the kitchen, wondering if he could get away with telling Todd that mango ice cream with freshly grated Parmesan cheese was the latest thing.

*　*　*

Hope went back to work as if nothing had happened. One of the girls asked if she had enjoyed her lunch, and she said yes. No one had noticed that she had left in Todd's car and come back in a taxi, although Mrs Potter eyed the dress she was still wearing with fresh disapproval.

She was finding it hard to believe that Todd had expected her to spy on Finn. She didn't want a new house that much. In fact, she didn't want a new house at all. She liked her little cottage.

Suddenly, the idea of being married to Todd didn't seem appealing at all. She would spend her days in a house she hated — and she knew she was going to hate it — trying to get pregnant before it was too late, and if the children were anything like their father she would probably hate them as well. That thought made her smile. Did mothers ever hate their children? Probably not, but the thought of a load of little Todds running around certainly made her shudder.

She drove home to her cottage thinking about what she wanted from the rest of her life. She hardly knew Finn and he hadn't made any promises, but right this moment anything seemed better than a life as Mrs Bartlett. She took a deep breath. This was going to be entirely up to her.

Taking a bottle of supermarket white wine out of her fridge, she poured herself a generous glass. It was unlikely that Todd would be home from the

Country Club yet. He would be telling his buddies it was her time of the month and they would be discussing the tantrums of their various wives and girlfriends and laughing together, probably over a glass of the best wine the Country Club could provide.

Hope finished her quite nice Chardonnay, changed into jeans, and went out into her tiny back yard to plant the roses she had bought at the nursery. They were miniatures, which the nurseryman had told her would be perfect for a small garden, and with their tiny pink buds they matched her bedspread too. Next year, when they'd had time to become established, she would pick a few buds to put in a vase on her dressing table.

She sat back on her heels. If she married Todd, she wouldn't be living here next year, and her roses would belong to someone else. Students who would have parties in her garden and throw cigarette butts on the flowerbed.

And if she moved to the house Todd

was going to have built, he would employ a garden designer who probably wouldn't like roses either.

She was in the kitchen washing the earth off her hands when the doorbell rang. This time Todd didn't wait to be asked in. He walked past her and stood facing her from across the room.

'I hope you're feeling better now. I don't appreciate being made to look a fool in front of my friends.'

They weren't his friends. They were merely people who liked being seen with someone who owned several companies and drove an expensive car, and if he had just come over to tell her off, he could jolly well leave.

When she didn't answer him, he sat down on her shabby sofa. 'I spoke to my mother. She said you were suffering from pre-wedding nerves. Nothing to be ashamed off, but you can't let nerves get the better of you.

'My mother is handling all the wedding arrangements, so all you have to do is relax and enjoy yourself. Find something useful to do. Choose furniture for the house, if that's what you want — I'm sure there will be some pieces we agree on — and decide what sort of wedding dress you want to wear. My mother has already contacted a few designers on your behalf.'

He came towards her and she backed away a few steps. 'I want you to be happy, Hope. Forget Finn Masters — I'll get a professional to investigate him. We'll find out his weak spots and make him an offer he can't refuse. You'll still get your house.'

Knowing it would be quite impossible to forget Finn Masters, she waited to make quite sure he had finished before she spoke.

'I'm not going to marry you, Todd. We've both changed, and we don't seem to want the same things any more.'

'Nerves,' Todd repeated dismissively. 'All women have pre-wedding nerves. It was all just a dream before, wasn't it? But now you know it's a reality and it's actually going to happen, you're bound to be nervous.'

Hope didn't feel nervous — she felt scared. She had just seen the rest of her life flash before her eyes.

'Tell your mother I'm sorry, but I can't go through with all this. I know you find it hard to believe, Todd, but I don't want your kind of life. I don't want a big house. I like my little cottage — and I quite like living on my own.'

'You can't put the wedding off, Hope. Plans have been made, but you've got plenty of time to get over this nonsense and start co-operating. You have to realise you can't always stamp your feet and get your own way.'

He looked at his watch. 'I've got a meeting in half an hour. The world isn't going to stop because you're having a hissy fit. Think about it — we've been together for years. If you'd had any real doubts, you'd have realised it before now.'

She kept quiet while he kissed her on

the cheek and let himself out. He was right, of course — she should have realised it before now — but thank goodness the light had eventually dawned. What if she had actually married this man? A man she had just discovered was a complete stranger!

At some point she needed to warn Finn that he had been threatened. It was becoming a battle of the houses — and if someone was going to lose, it wouldn't be Todd.

Surprised to find that she was hungry, she made cheese on toast and ate it with another glass of wine. Noticing the ostentatious ring on her finger, she tried to pull it off. It moved only as far as her knuckle and stuck tight.

Once she had finished eating she soaped her finger and slid the ring off. The diamond was quite big, but it was set in platinum and she preferred gold. He would have known that, if he'd asked her. His mother had probably chosen the ring, and by now she would have the wedding dress picked out, the invitations ordered, and the bridesmaids sorted by height.

Feeling much better without the weight of the ring on her finger, she turned on the television and settled down on her sofa.

★   ★   ★

The bell must have rung several times before she heard it, but now it had become one continuous ring. Someone had their finger pressed against the button. Hope hesitated, fearing Todd had come back for another go at her, but the noise got the better of her and she opened the door.

Todd's mother looked as if she had just come from the hairdresser. She was wearing a summery dress in beige with a silky cardigan to match, and Hope wondered how the woman always managed to look so elegant.

Wiping her hands nervously on her jeans, Hope held the door open.

'I've just finished eating, but please come in.'

Fiona Bartlett walked into Hope's living room and reduced it to a shack with one sweep of her critical eyes.

'Todd was right, it is very small.' She smiled. 'Quaint. Perfect for a young girl on her own, but not big enough for a married couple.'

'No,' Hope said.

'Todd telephoned me. He's worried about you.' Mrs Bartlett took a tissue out of her bag and brushed the seat of the chair before she sat down. 'An attack of nerves at this late date is a bit selfish, don't you think?'

Hope sat primly on her sofa. She felt like a naughty schoolgirl.

'This is not an attack of nerves,' she said calmly. 'I meant it when I told Todd I cannot marry him. It's better for him to find out now. He would be even more upset if I changed my mind halfway down the aisle.'

'You're being quite ridiculous, Hope. The arrangements are well under way.

You can't back out now.'

Is that what I am doing, she wondered, *backing out?*

Hope picked up the ring from where it lay on the coffee table. 'Perhaps you wouldn't mind returning this to Todd for me. I'm sure he will be able to get his money back.'

Fiona Bartlett stood up. 'You'll regret this, Hope. I can't believe there's another man involved, so I can only assume that you think this little tantrum will get you your own way. Todd told me about your ridiculous idea of a picnic in a field.' She dropped the ring into her Prada handbag. 'Just be careful, my girl. Todd won't put up with this silly behaviour much longer.'

Hope didn't move when the front door slammed. That woman might have become her mother-in-law — a thought that was almost as frightening as the idea of spending the rest of her life with Todd.

5

Hope slept badly. Ending a relationship that had gone on for so long was like getting a divorce. She was now quite sure that she didn't want to spend the rest of her life with Todd, but she still felt lost without him.

The workday dragged. Todd didn't call, and neither did Finn, and at five o'clock Hope left the office and drove home slowly through the rush-hour traffic. Living on your own was fine when you had someone to take you out occasionally and buy you a nice dinner, but realising you might be on your own for the rest of your life was quite scary.

Todd was a born organiser, and he had mapped out her whole life for her. Now she was going to have to think for herself.

As soon as she walked into her cottage, her spirits lifted and she realised life wasn't so bad. The little house was going to be hers forever — as long as she could pay the mortgage — and her roses would come up next year without having to fear for their lives.

But she still had to warn Finn. She knew what Todd was capable of. He wouldn't back down over anything, and it was partly his sheer persistence that had got him where he was. He wanted the house he had helped to design, built on the plot of land he had chosen, and he wasn't likely to take no for an answer. In fact, she thought bitterly, Todd Bartlett simply didn't understand what the word 'No' meant.

She still had no idea what Finn's mobile number was. There was only one thing for it; she would have to drive round to his house and hope he was in.

Quickly changing from her navy skirt and white blouse into comfy jeans and trainers, she made herself a quick snack of pasta and salad, and then jumped into her car and drove to the manor house.

By the time she arrived it was already quite dark. She pulled up on the weed-studded drive and sat in her car without moving. She had no idea what she was going to say to Finn. This seemed to be her week for indecisiveness. She had come to warn him about Todd's threat, but if she was honest with herself, that wasn't the only reason. She desperately wanted to see Finn again, which was quite ridiculous since she had only known him a few days.

Before she could get her thoughts in order, the front door opened and Finn stood there, looking at her. She felt her heart literally miss a beat — something she had thought only happened in romantic novels.

He walked over and opened the door of her car.

'Are you just going to sit there, or are you coming inside?'

Silently she got out and followed him

into the house's dimly-lit hallway.

'I came to warn you, Finn. Todd is going to make sure you sell the house. It sounded like a threat to me.'

He frowned. 'And this should worry me?'

She took a breath. 'I don't know, perhaps not — but Todd plays dirty, particularly if he thinks he won't get what he wants, and he wants this house — or rather, the land it's sitting on. I think he's already invested money on the assumption the land will be available.'

Finn took her arm gently and led her into the kitchen. 'Then that's his problem, isn't it? I never told anyone I was definitely selling — only that I was prepared to look at offers. That was before I read my grandmother's letter.'

Hope sat on a kitchen chair. 'So you've decided not to sell?'

He waved a hand at a stack of paint cans in the corner. 'I've got these on sale or return, and I've got loads of paint charts. I was hoping you'd help me choose the right colours for the different rooms.'

She beamed excitedly at him. 'You want me to help? Oh, Finn, I'd love to.' She was already on her feet, lifting the cans and looking at the colours. 'I can help you paint, as well. I'm now an experienced decorator. It's not as hard as I thought it would be.'

He came up behind her and rested his hands lightly on her shoulders. She could feel his breath on her cheek as she turned to face him.

'Are you still promised to Todd Bartlett, Hope?'

She smiled at his quaint use of language. Almost without thinking, she followed her longing, reached up and kissed him lightly on the lips.

'No, I'm not promised to anyone. I broke up with Todd last night. He didn't believe me, though, and neither did his mother. They both think I'm having a bad case of pre-wedding nerves.'

'And are you?'

She smiled into his eyes. 'What do you think?'

He pulled her into his arms and kissed her with enough passion to make her toes curl and waves of pleasure surge through her whole body. What seemed like several minutes later, he drew away.

'I'm not going to say anything right now that I might regret later. You need time to think this through and make quite sure you know what you're doing.' He kissed her more gently, and then held her at arm's length. 'At the moment I have nothing to offer you. I have a temporary job, I'm in debt, and I may well lose this house, however hard I try to keep it. I'm not a good trade-in for a millionaire who could give you everything you want.'

'I don't want everything.' She nearly added 'except you', but that was probably too much, too soon. Finn was right — she was on the rebound at the moment, and that wasn't fair to him.

'I agree, you're a lousy trade-in,' she

said lightly, 'but a trade-in's not what I want, either. So we play it cool for a bit, yes?'

When he dropped his hands from her shoulders, she smiled. 'How about that tour of the cellar?'

As Hope followed him down the cellar steps, she said regretfully, 'What a pity you had to sell all your grandmother's furniture. Some of it was really beautiful — it just needed restoring.'

Finn switched on a torch and shone it on the worn stone steps. 'Mind how you go. I can't promise to catch you a second time, and there's no light down here.' When they reached the bottom, he turned to face her. 'I had to sell everything, Hope. I've always lived in rented accommodation, so I had nothing else — no other way of raising the money for the inheritance tax.'

'Have you paid it all now?'

'No, I'm still a few thousand short, and the bank won't give me a loan because they know the house could take years to sell to a private buyer. I'm not going to give it away.' He turned his face away. 'Grandma deserved more than that.'

Hope had to practically run down the remaining steps to catch up with him. She was dying to ask more questions, but he had already moved ahead of her with his torch, leaving her standing in the dark at the bottom of the stairs. She thought she heard a rustling somewhere behind her, and hurried towards the beam of light.

The cellar was amazing. It ran right across the width of the house and looked more solid than the building above. As Finn swung the torch around she saw the floor was made of earth, packed tight by the tread of hundreds of feet over the years, and brick arches held up the roof, sending strange shadows flitting across the walls. Hope kept a wary eye out for rats, ready to behave like a girl and scream loudly if one should run across her feet. Surprisingly, the place didn't smell damp, and Finn told her it was kept dry by the movement of air through the vents high up near the ceiling.

'A perfect place to keep wine,' he said.

As they moved further into the cellar, where the shadows were deepest, something scuttled really quickly along the back wall. Hope didn't make a sound. It was Finn who let out a little yelp — she had clutched his bare arm tightly enough to cut off the circulation.

'It was a field mouse,' he told her, prising her fingers away from his arm. 'There's probably a nest in here somewhere.'

'A nest? Like lots of them? Lots of mice?'

'Yes, little baby mice who never hurt anyone. They need a home, same as everyone else.'

'Yes, but there's a clue in the name, Finn. Field mice. They're supposed to live in fields.'

'And barns, and anywhere else where they can keep warm and dry. The temperature down here is probably just about right for them. Cool, but not actually cold.'

Another rustle made Hope shudder. 'Can we go now?' she asked shakily. 'I think I've seen enough.'

He led the way back up to the kitchen and filled the kettle. 'I'll make coffee and we'll take it into the library. It's more comfortable in there.'

'No — let's stay in here. I want to look at your paint charts. There's a firm that makes heritage paints, where you can get the same colours that were used in the Victorian era. They're a lot more expensive, but we might be able to match them with cheaper versions from one of the DIY stores and keep the colours more or less authentic.'

'I need to clean the place up first,' he said, 'before I even think about painting. I've got a mop and bucket. Do I need anything else?'

She laughed. 'I'll make you a list. Can I come over after work and help? I really want to. It will take my mind off . . . other things.'

'We can't paint in the dark, but I suppose we can clean.' He handed her a sheet of paper and a pencil. 'Make your list. I'll leave work early tomorrow and go shopping.'

'And I'll come round after work, but I'll have to go home and change first. My office get-up isn't exactly suitable for cleaning a house.'

'You can change here, surely.'

She raised an eyebrow and he laughed. 'Maybe not. If I'm having trouble with temptation at the moment, goodness knows what would happen if I saw you in your undies.'

'Don't worry, it won't happen.'

Not yet, anyway, she thought to herself, but the mere idea brought a flush to her cheeks and made her heart beat a little faster. This delightful feeling of light-headedness had never happened when she was with Todd — or maybe it had, once, but if so she had forgotten all about it.

She gulped coffee that was still too hot and spluttered, feeling stupid. She had to regain control of herself. She didn't want to become one of those women who could not exist without a man. She wanted to prove to herself that she could be independent before she got involved with anyone else — and Finn seemed happy enough to take things slowly.

Looking at him now, as he lounged back on the hard wooden chair, his long legs stretched out in front of him, she wondered whose resolve was going to crack first.

She wrote him a list of cleaning products and they studied the colour charts, choosing colours that seemed suitable for the large rooms. Finn had drawn a plan of the garden, hoping one day to restore it to its former beauty.

'If we can get the house cleaned and painted,' she said encouragingly, 'and the garden tidied up, I'm sure someone will want to buy it.'

'If we have time. There are still a lot of bills that need to be paid. During the last few months of her life Grandma just put all the bills in a drawer unopened. I'm still going through them.'

'Haven't you got a solicitor to help you?' she asked. He laughed ruefully.

'I did have, but he was costing too much money. Catch twenty-two. Now I'm trying to fix things on my own.'

Impulsively, she caught his hand. 'You're not on your own, Finn. There are two of us now.'

★　★　★

He watched from the front door until her car disappeared from view. He didn't like her driving in the dark, but she was a grown woman — he had no doubts about that — and he had to stop treating her like a child.

Shutting the heavy front door, he was suddenly quite glad of its sturdy bolts top and bottom. What did Todd Bartlett's threat mean? he wondered. Surely a man of Todd's standing wouldn't involve himself in something as stupid as physical violence.

He threw together a meal made from Country Club leftovers, and then booted up his laptop. Hope seemed to think Todd was already involved in a deal concerning the manor house — a house that didn't belong to him.

How could that happen? Finn wondered.

A check of all current planning applications didn't throw up anything, but he hadn't expected that it would.

He went to the fridge and pulled out a beer, drinking the cold liquid straight from the bottle. Hope had said Todd stood to lose a lot of money if the sale of the house didn't go through — and Todd wasn't the kind of man to lie about money. He didn't need to.

Finn shut down the computer and picked up the phone. He still had friends in town. Friends he could call on when he needed them. Usually he paid them back with a gourmet meal cooked in their own home, and the slate was wiped clean.

Joe Faraday was an Internet wizard and promised to have the information Finn wanted by the following day.

'Hack into the Town Hall computers?' he asked. 'I thought you were wanting me to do something difficult.'

Finn smiled as he put the phone down. There was no way he was going to sell the house. Not to anyone. Todd Bartlett might be a clever businessman, but as Finn had discovered long ago, you don't need to be clever — you just need to have clever friends.

* * *

Hope turned up faithfully at the house every evening for the rest of the week. She drove home from work, changed into old jeans and a paint-splattered top and drove to Finn's, where she proceeded to clean and sweep until dusk, when working in the dimly-lit house became practically impossible.

Once the big room was really clean, Finn wanted to start painting. Hope felt that after finishing the walls in her own house, she was a master of the art, but the main room covered an area that was twice the size of the whole of the ground floor in her little cottage. Quite a daunting task — and the ceilings were so high they would be difficult to reach at all.

Cleaning the house showed up its deficiencies. Woodwork that would have to be replaced, broken windows, guttering filled with birds' nests, and crumbling plaster that would need a professional to put it right. The electrics were positively dangerous and the plumbing was antiquated. Finn wanted to keep the bathroom fittings where possible, and Hope got stuck in with a long-handled brush and large quantities of cleaning fluid. She had the bright idea of filling the toilet bowls practically to the brim with fresh water and then adding bleach followed by scale remover. Left for several hours, her tactics worked pretty well.

By the end of the week, the garden

was beginning to look less of a wilderness. The paving slabs on the patio turned out to be Italian marble and practically indestructible, and Finn found a couple of old stone urns hidden in the bushes. They would eventually go either side of the front door and be filled with seasonal flowers.

Hope loved working with Finn. He trusted her to get on with whatever task she had chosen, and never queried her judgement — quite the contrary, he often asked for her ideas and took them on board. She was happier than she had ever been in her life.

On the Saturday Finn worked a double shift, so Hope spent the day on her own at the cottage. Every time the doorbell rang, she jumped and looked fearfully out of her front window. She was sure Todd would call round at some point.

She had made a few rough sketches of the garden at the old house, and spent the morning drawing a diagram of the various areas around the house so that when Finn eventually got around to planting, perhaps in the spring, he would know where everything needed to go.

She didn't want to admit, even to herself, how much she missed him.

6

The first thing Hope heard on Sunday morning was the ringing of the phone. She glanced at her bedside clock. It was barely seven o'clock. Who would be ringing her this early? Her alarm wouldn't go off for another hour and she begrudged losing her sleep. But when she heard the voice in her ear, she smiled.

'Oh — good morning, Finn. It's a bit early for me. I usually have a lie-in on a Sunday.'

'Oh, sorry — I've been up for ages. What are your plans for today?'

'I thought we were going to work on the house some more, or get on with clearing up the garden.'

'I was going to give you the day off. I don't expect you to work over here all the time like some sort of slave. The house is my responsibility.'

'Finn, I like working with you on the house, or I wouldn't come over.'

'Could you come over now, then, please?' he asked. 'Because I need to talk to someone.'

She swung her legs out of bed. 'Give me half an hour. Have you got anything for breakfast?' She listened to the silence. 'I'll pick up bacon and eggs on the way.'

She called in at the twenty-four-hour supermarket and picked up eggs and bacon, a loaf of bread, a pack of butter, and a pint of milk. She knew he had instant coffee and she remembered seeing a frying pan.

She drove out to the house with a lightness in her heart that she hadn't experienced for ages. For the last three years, she realised, she had been in a job she didn't like, engaged to a man she didn't love, and constantly made to feel guilty for being independent.

Taking one hand off the wheel, she pushed the button to open the sunroof. It was going to be a beautiful Sunday.

Finn greeted her with a smile that made her knees go weak.

'I'm sorry, I'm being incredibly selfish. You should be sleeping. The sun was up and I didn't realise how early it was.'

The kitchen door was open and she could see he had started pulling up the weeds and cleaning the flagstones on the little patio outside.

'You've already been busy.'

'I couldn't sleep. My head was buzzing with ideas. I keep thinking I'm going to find a way to stay here.'

'Didn't you make enough at the auction to pay most of the bills?'

He took bacon out of the pack she had brought and dropped it on to an already hot skillet that looked as if it was probably as old as the house.

'I'm still several thousand short, and that might as well be a couple of million. There's no way I can make up the deficit. I've sold everything I've got, apart from my car, and I need that.'

Just for a moment she actually

considered trying to raise money on her cottage — but she already had a hefty mortgage.

'What will you do?'

He scooped out the bacon, transferred it to a plate, and broke four eggs into the pan while she buttered slices of bread.

'That's why I wanted to talk to you. I've got one or two ideas, and I've had a letter from the builder. I'll show you when we've eaten.'

He had cleaned the downstairs windows and sunlight streamed into the kitchen, warming the big room. The weather was being kind at the moment, but Hope could easily imagine the house being quite cold and damp if the temperature dropped.

They ate in companionable silence, listening to the sound of the birds in the trees outside. When he stood up to make the coffee, Hope said, 'I haven't heard anything from Todd.'

Finn didn't answer for a moment. 'Does that bother you?'

'Not really, but I'm sure he won't just give up — so every day is like waiting for the other shoe to drop.'

He turned and smiled at her. 'I thought you might be missing him.'

She smiled back. 'How could I? I haven't had time. You've kept me too busy.' She took the coffee he handed her. 'Tell me what the builder said.'

He took a letter from the dresser and handed it to her. 'Read that.'

She looked up after a few moments. 'They're offering you a million pounds?'

'Yes, and the house, together with the land it stands on, is only valued at seven hundred thousand. They really want this place, don't they?'

'Do you have an alternative?'

He picked up the mugs and put them in the sink.

'When I went to the bank to ask for money and they practically laughed in my face, I noticed there was a poster that said they were giving loans for small businesses.'

She looked round the kitchen. Even

though the house was a lot cleaner than it had been, the rooms still looked bare. 'What sort of business could you run from here?'

'I could turn it into a restaurant.'

She stared at him. 'I know you've always wanted your own restaurant, Finn, but you'd need more than a million just to get started.'

'No.' He shook his head. 'Nothing like that. If I thought there was a chance of making a go of it, I could do a lot of the work myself. As for the restaurant side, I know all the suppliers, and where I can get really good quality meat and vegetables.' He ran a hand through his hair. 'I just need the time.'

She picked up the letter from the builder. 'You'd give up the chance of a million pounds?'

'In a blink. Just think about it, Hope. I only need to do up a couple of rooms and the garden. There's no need to bother about the upstairs — not to begin with, anyway. The kitchen will have to be fitted out, but I know plenty of people who can do that for me at cost price. I can get enough tables in the main room to be sure of a steady profit, and I can open the doors in the summer and put more tables outside.' He spun round. 'All I need is a really good proposal to put before the bank.'

Feeling like a party-pooper, Hope said gently, 'They may still turn you down, you know.'

'No they won't.' He grinned at her. 'How could they turn down such a brilliant idea? If it hadn't been for you telling me I mustn't sell, and helping me clean the place up, I would never have thought of turning this place into a restaurant.' He took her face between his hands and kissed her gently on the lips. 'Thank you, Hope. I love you.'

She felt the heat in her face. He didn't mean it, of course, it was just a form of speech, but her heart was racing so fast she wondered how she would she feel if he really did mean it. Fainting like a Victorian heroine was a distinct possibility.

'So where do I fit in?' she asked.

He took both her hands in his and looked into her eyes. 'Do you really want to be part of this?'

'You can't tell me you love me and then shut me out,' she said lightly. 'Of course I want to be part of it. Where do we start?'

'With drawings, I think. I know an architect who might be prepared to help. Meanwhile we can carry on tidying the place up.' He pulled open a drawer and took out a folder. 'The trouble is, they expect me to pay the inheritance tax with the proceeds from the sale of the house, and I don't know how long I can stall.'

Hope showed Finn her drawing of the garden and they walked around in the sunshine, planning where everything would go. Finn wanted to extend the back terrace and cover it in some way so it could be used all year round, and Hope suggested a small play area for children so that their parents could eat in peace.

They took chairs out on to the patio for lunch; Hope made cheese and bacon sandwiches while Finn opened a couple of bottles of cold beer. Afterwards, he made a start on designing his perfect kitchen while Hope reworked her garden plan.

She took a pad and pencil and walked round the grounds, making notes of plants she wanted to keep and those that would have to go. Everything needed to be child-friendly, so she wanted to check for any poisonous plants that would have to be removed.

She reminded him that they would need toilet facilities on the ground floor, and he decided the library could be converted as long as the plumbing wouldn't cost too much. His architect friend could advise him on that. It was only when it became difficult to see that Hope realised how long she had been at the house. It really had been a perfect day.

'I have to go home, Finn,' she told him. 'I have to see Todd at some point,

I can't just ignore him. I think I may have treated him rather badly, suddenly telling him the wedding was off. We've been together for a long time and he deserved more than that. If he doesn't come round to see me tonight, I'll try and sort things out tomorrow once and for all.'

'Do you still love him, Hope?'

'No — I think I fell out of love with him some time ago. We sort of grew apart and we're both different people now.' She looked at Finn, a little fearfully. 'I just don't want to make any more mistakes.'

He smiled as he held open the front door.

'Believe me, Hope — I may be a lot of things, but I'm not a mistake.'

When she got home she checked her phone messages but Todd still hadn't called. She wasn't sure whether he was trying to punish her or giving her time to get over her silliness. Either way, she knew he wouldn't let her go without a fight. It wasn't in his nature. He always got what he wanted, and she wasn't about to become the exception to the rule.

* * *

She walked into the office on Monday morning a little nervously, thinking someone might have heard of her break-up with Todd, but everything seemed perfectly normal. Someone did mention the fact that she wasn't wearing her engagement ring, but she evaded the issue by saying it kept sliding off her finger and needed to be a size smaller.

'Wedding nerves,' one of the girls said. 'Makes you lose weight.'

Someone else laughed. 'A diet is a whole lot easier.'

Hope wondered why she hadn't just told the truth — it was bound to come out in the end — but first she needed to make Todd understand that this wasn't just some strange aberration on her part.

By lunchtime she'd had enough. She dialled Todd on her office phone.

'Hello,' he said brightly. 'How are you feeling? I thought I'd give you a bit of space to sort yourself out. I know you didn't mean what you said. I've had a word with my mother and we've come up with a few ideas to make things easier for you. Not so stressful.'

Hope felt as if she was banging her head against the proverbial wall, and it hurt just as much. Todd was never going to believe she had actually finished with him and for a moment she was at a loss. She had no idea what to do next.

'I need to talk to you, Todd,' she said. 'Can you meet me for lunch?'

'Of course,' he said, 'but there's no need to apologise. I've got the ring with me.' He chuckled down the phone. 'I didn't think you'd really want to give back a diamond that size.'

By the time she arrived at the restaurant she had come to a decision. There was only one way out. Barely giving him time to sit down, she said, 'I've met someone else.'

He stared at her for so long she almost took her words back and told him it was just a joke — but then she realised the look on his face wasn't heartbreak, it was total disbelief. He actually laughed at her.

'Hope, this is ridiculous. I can understand you being nervous, and I know my mother can be a little overwhelming at times, but telling me a pack of lies won't help. Don't you think I'd have known about it if you'd really met someone else?'

'I'm not lying,' she said quietly.

Completely ignoring what she had just said, he pulled his chair closer to the table and put his hand over hers.

'Like I told you, I discussed it with my mother and we decided a spring wedding would be possible. No point in waiting until the autumn if we don't have to. All the arrangements are already on board, anyway, but I'll meet you halfway and agree to us being married in that little church by the river you like so much.' He smiled and squeezed her hand. 'No big scary cathedral or anything — just a few friends and family.'

Mostly his *friends and family*, she thought bitterly as she resolutely pulled her hand away.

'I really have met someone else, Todd, so the wedding is off. Please tell your mother to cancel any arrangements she has already made. I was worried about hurting you, but I now don't think that would be possible.'

She already had her handbag and jacket, so she collected her car from the office car park and drove home. She didn't realise she was weeping until her tears dripped on to her lap.

She had no idea why she was crying. Possibly because life as she knew it had just ended, and she was scared to death. For some time she had felt that her life needed shaking up, but this was going a little bit further than she had intended.

She made herself a cheese and lettuce sandwich and a cup of tea, and wrote an email to her boss. Lying through her teeth, she said she had a sudden toothache and needed to see a dentist, but would be back at work tomorrow and hoped she wasn't inconveniencing anyone too much.

The only person she was really inconveniencing, she thought darkly, was Todd's mother. The designer wedding suit would have to go into storage until Todd married someone else, which she was quite sure he would do. He wanted a wife, and his mother wanted grandchildren — but just who ended up providing those services didn't really matter to either of them.

Feeling a lot better with some food inside her, she changed into jeans and a baggy top, swapped her heels for flat sandals, and drove round to Finn's house, hoping he was on an early shift. She was surprised to see another car parked in the driveway.

Finn drove a two-year-old black

saloon. Now it had been joined by a sleek red sports car.

Thinking he was bound to have the kitchen door open, she walked round the back of the house, curious to see who his visitor was.

Two people were sitting at the kitchen table. A girl with long blonde hair, red lipstick, and very white teeth — and Finn. They had a bottle on the table, glasses in front of them, and they were both laughing at something they obviously found highly amusing.

Hope stood still for a moment, not moving. Finn didn't have a sister or any other female relations, as far as she could recall — but he could invite anyone he liked to his own house, it was none of her business. So why did she feel so put out?

'Hello,' she said in a neutral voice.

Finn turned, still laughing, and the woman looked at Hope and then back at Finn questioningly.

'You're early,' he said. 'Good. You're just in time to hear Josie's ideas. She's the architect I was telling you about. Josie, this is Hope.'

'I've heard a lot about you, too,' Josie said.

Hope wanted to crawl away and find a hole to hide in. Beauty and brains in one package was too much for her. She simply couldn't compete. The woman was wearing a pale grey trouser suit that accentuated her curves, and Greek sandals in the same colour on slender feet. Hope felt like a bag lady in contrast.

There wasn't anywhere for her to sit, so she stood awkwardly just inside the door, wishing she had stayed at home. Finn got up so that she could have his chair, and Josie spread some drawings out on the table.

'These are only rough sketches,' she told Hope. 'And since Finn tells me I have to keep costs to the minimum, we may have to re-think some of my ideas. The house isn't listed, so that's one headache out of the way, and after a quick look round, the building appears sound. It's built of brick, so planning permission for internal alterations shouldn't pose any problems.'

Hope wasn't listening. She had seen the way Finn was looking at Josie. He looked really proud of her.

'Have you seen the bank manager?' she asked him.

He shook his head. 'Not yet. I've made an appointment for the end of the week. By then, Josie will have scale drawings for me.'

A sudden burst of noise made both women jump. Reaching into his pocket, Finn grinned at them. His phone was playing the *Crazy Frog* tune.

'Sorry,' he said apologetically. 'I never got around to changing it.'

Hope and Josie watched his face change as he listened to the caller.

'Is that a threat? Okay, I'll read it again, but I won't be rushed into this. It's a big decision.' He put the phone back in his pocket. 'That was the builder who wants to buy this land. He suggested I read his letter again and make a note of the amount I'm being offered, because it would be very silly to turn it down.'

Josie frowned. 'If the plans for the estate are at the Town Hall already, you've got a problem. The builders are going to start losing money if building is delayed. They must have assumed you were going to sell.'

'Well, they assumed wrong — and no plans have been submitted. I checked that.'

'Fine,' Josie said, gathering up her drawings. 'Just don't sign anything.'

'She seems nice,' Hope said, as they watched Josie swing her little car round and drive away.

'She is.' Finn smiled at her. 'We've been friends for years. You don't have to worry.'

'About what?' Hope felt her face grow hot. 'I wasn't worried about anything. Like I said, she seems nice.'

Finn's smile widened. 'And like I said, she is.'

7

Finn went outside to pull up some more weeds, and as Hope was dressed for work she set about cleaning up the kitchen, the only room that hadn't had a thorough going-over. The floor had already been swept, but she found a mop and a bucket and gave the quarry tiles a good wash.

She was trying to poke the mop behind the heavy wooden dresser when something scuttled over her feet and disappeared beneath the cellar door.

Her shriek was muted by terror, coming out as a squeak so small that even a mouse would have been ashamed of it, but Finn was by her side in moments.

'What's the matter?'

'Mice!' she said with a shudder. 'Well, a mouse. It ran over my foot. We have to get rid of them, Finn. A health inspector would have a field day.'

'They'll go when we get the place properly cleaned up.'

She shook her head. 'No they won't. They've already colonised your cellar — hundreds of them, probably. They must come up here to eat.'

'I think you're exaggerating,' Finn said easily. 'An old place like this will always have a few mice.'

'But not a restaurant. Mice count as vermin, like rats. You have to get rid of them before anyone comes to look round.'

He smiled, rinsing his hands under the tap to get rid of the mud. 'Fancy another trip down to the cellar?'

'Do I have to come?'

'You're the one who's complaining. I can live with a few mice, but I'm obviously more altruistic than you.'

'If you open your restaurant, you can give them a table all to themselves for all I care, but you won't get that far if the place is crawling with vermin.'

He came and put his arm round her.

'Mummy mice, Hope, with little baby mice, a whole community that have probably lived here for years and years. Are you suggesting we commit genocide?'

She wriggled away from him. 'Have you ever seen baby mice? They look like big maggots until they get fur. And no, I'm not suggesting we kill off the whole species, just the ones in your cellar.'

He rubbed his hands together. 'Let's do it, then. What do we needs? A machete? A machine gun?'

Ignoring him, she picked up the torch he had left on the windowsill and flung open the door to the cellar. Starting down the stairs, she kept the beam focused on her feet. Trainers would have been more sensible than sandals. The feel of those tiny feet on her bare skin had been truly horrible.

Silence greeted them in the cellar. No patter of feet. No scratching noises in the shadows.

'Give me the torch, Hope,' Finn said. 'We need to look for holes in the brickwork, anywhere they might nest.'

A close inspection of the walls failed to reveal any holes. The floor was solid as well, but Finn found a wide ledge in a corner covered with droppings.

'This looks like it.' He used the torch to investigate further. 'There are some old bottles stacked one on top of the other — and what looks like a mouse nest behind them.' He looked around for something solid and found a piece of lead pipe. 'This should do the job.'

Hope caught hold of his arm. 'Wait a minute. If you start poking at the nest with that, you'll have mice running everywhere, and if you break the bottles we'll have broken glass to clear up as well.'

Finn ignored her and moved closer. Hearing scuttling, she backed away while he shone the torch into the dark space. The sickly sweet stench of mice made her hold her nose. Finn used the pipe to poke gingerly behind the bottles and several mice ran down the wall, disappearing into the dark.

'The shelf is full of rubbish,' he said. 'Bits of cardboard and paper, cloth from somewhere,' he poked some more, 'and goodness knows what else. It might be an idea to move the bottles and set light to the rest of the junk.'

'Now who's talking about genocide?' She wanted the mice gone, but not burned alive. How could anyone live with that on their conscience? 'What if you pull out some of the garbage and leave the nest exposed for a few days? They might decide to move house.'

'Yes, but where to? We don't want them moving in upstairs with us. I know — I'll get a load of those humane traps and dot them around the cellar. We may not get them all, but hopefully enough so I can clean out the nest.'

Hope laughed softly. 'You don't actually want to stick your hand in there any more than I do, do you?'

'I tell you what would be really nice,' he said, taking her arm and leading her up the cellar steps. 'A couple of beers at the local pub.'

* * *

On the Friday evening, five days after Hope had told Todd she wasn't going to marry him, he arrived on her doorstep.

'You look well for someone getting over a failed relationship,' he said sarcastically, when she answered the door.

She kept the door half closed. 'What do you want, Todd?'

'I know who Lover Boy is, and he's not for you — you must realise that. A penniless yob squatting in a house he's going to have to sell. He got an offer well over what the house is worth. Tell him to take it — because it won't be around much longer.'

Still keeping the door half closed, she asked, 'How do you know how much Finn was offered?'

Todd ignored her question. 'I've already said I'll let you have your own way over the wedding. What more do you want?'

What she wanted, Hope realised, was passion. Something intense and mind-blowing. Not being able to breathe when he was near, feeling her heart race uncontrollably if he accidentally touched her hand, wanting to be with him every minute of every day. She had never thought those things were possible, but now she knew they were. Not just in her imagination, but real.

'We were friends once, Todd, but that's all we ever were. We enjoyed one another's company — to begin with, anyway — but that isn't enough for me. You asked what more I want, and it's something you can't give me.'

He waved a hand disdainfully. 'So you choose this, do you? A cottage not big enough to swing a cat, and the company of some kitchen boy who's squatting in a derelict house?'

'I think you'd better go, Todd.'

'I'll be watching you, Hope, and your new boyfriend, and when you realise how stupid you're being, you're going to beg me to take you back. What do you think you're you going to live on? Love?'

That might be possible, she thought, as she closed the door. Talking to Todd had made her realise she was in love with Finn. Now all she had to do was convince him her relationship with Todd was really over.

★   ★   ★

Hope woke to a Saturday that was sunny and warm, so she dressed in shorts, a sleeveless top and sandals, tying her hair back in a ponytail. Finn had told her again to take Saturday off, but she needed to see him. She didn't think Todd would do anything violent, but he didn't like being beaten, and she worried he might try and get back at Finn in some way.

Thinking Finn might be having a lie-in, now that his bedroom was clean and comfortable, she made herself eat breakfast before she drove to the house.

Her heart sank when she saw the red car in the driveway. What was Josie doing here?

The first thing she heard as she made her way round the back of the house was the sound of laughter. *Josie must be a very amusing woman*, she thought, as she stepped up on to the patio. The kitchen door was open, the remains of breakfast spread out on the table. Josie was the first to look up.

'I thought you were taking the day off, Hope.'

Hope couldn't think what to say. She couldn't tell Finn about her concerns in front of Josie. The sight of the cosy little breakfast had thrown her completely. Had the woman been there all night? If not, she must have arrived pretty early.

'Hello, Josie. I just dropped by because I needed to speak to Finn.'

Josie stood up. 'I'm just going. Have a nice day, both of you.' She bent down and kissed Finn on the cheek. 'See you soon, lover.'

Hope watched the woman walk away, high heels clicking on the tiles, hair falling to her shoulders in golden waves, and felt sick. If this was the competition, she didn't stand a chance. She saw Finn grinning at her and felt the blood rush to her face. Was she that obvious?

'Todd came round yesterday,' she said, watching Finn's smile fade. 'He knows where you live and he says he'll be watching us. I just thought you ought to know.'

'So you're still seeing him.'

'No.' She shook her head. 'I'm well and truly over him. I don't want to see him again, ever — but he was quite nasty this time. Threatening. And I'm just worried he might try and do something to stop me seeing you.'

She could feel tears in her eyes and brushed a hand across her face.

'He knows a lot of important people.'

Finn had taken her in his arms before she realised what was happening. 'So do I,' he said against her hair. 'And you're one person who's very important to me, Hope Brown. I won't let him hurt you.'

She didn't think Todd would hurt her, but she clung to Finn like a child with a security blanket. With him, she felt utterly safe. She turned her head to look up at him and saw his pupils dilate.

There was nothing just-good-friends about this kiss. He lifted her up, and her feet left the ground as she wrapped her arms around his neck and their lips sought each other's hungrily and greedily. Her overwhelming feeling was that she had come home. This was where she belonged.

He set her back on the floor and brushed the tears from her face. 'Don't say anything you don't mean, Hope,' he said huskily. 'I want you to be really sure before you say anything. Just a couple of weeks ago you were engaged to another man . . . ' He put a finger on her lips when she tried to protest. 'Yes, you were, and I don't want you on the rebound. I want you all to myself.'

She could think of a lot of things she wanted to say to Finn, but first she needed to make sure Todd wasn't going to cause any trouble.

'So what did Josie want?'

He laughed. 'She came to tell me the plans I need for the bank manager are on my computer. She had to come early because she's away over the weekend.' This time his smile was wicked. 'She's going off on holiday with her husband and two children. Josie used to work for a hotel chain, that's how I met her.'

Hope sat down at the table and Finn poured her a cup of coffee. Then he booted up his laptop. The plans were really good; exactly what they wanted without being too drastic. The hallway had been widened and now had an archway leading into the main room, which, in turn, led to the kitchen. Josie had also managed to find space for a cloakroom with toilets on the ground floor, and suggested they replace the old, glazed doors to the terrace with concertina doors that would make the garden part of the living space.

'The doors will be double-glazed, but handmade in wood so they stay in keeping with the house. I told Josie I don't want a single piece of PVC anywhere. If we have to cut corners it will be somewhere it doesn't show.'

'Talking of corners,' Hope said, 'how are the mice?'

'Dwindling in numbers. Only one has to be re-homed today. If we go to the village for lunch, we can drop it off somewhere near the pub, and maybe tackle the nest later on.'

Hope shuddered. She knew the corner where the bottles were stored had to be cleaned out, but she intended standing well back while the job was done. They hoped to start painting on Monday, and the mice needed to go before then. Hope could imagine finding tiny footprints on the window-sills.

They took an hour for lunch, and let the mouse out of the trap near an old barn where it would most likely meet a new mate. The little creature stood in the open trap for a moment, looking at her with bright eyes, before it made its escape. Finn took her hand and they walked along the riverbank before driving back to the house.

* * *

After the sunlight, the cellar seemed darker than ever, a blackness that the torch hardly penetrated. Finn gave Hope the torch to hold and she aimed it at the recess. She didn't want to look, but if she shut her eyes she couldn't see where to point the torch. Once Finn had put on a pair of gardening gloves, he began pulling the rubbish out of the opening and dropping it into a bin bag. He put his hand behind the bottles, feeling around.

'Nothing moving around in here, and nothing has run past us, so I think they've all gone. I'll move the bottles and then we can brush down the shelf.' He picked up a filthy bottle and shone the torch on it. 'I reckon Grandfather kept a secret hoard my grandmother didn't know about. I remember my mother saying Grandma didn't like him drinking. Perhaps alcoholism runs in the family.'

'You don't drink much,' she observed, taking the bottle from him.

'Because alcohol killed my mother. She drove into a wall while she was blind drunk. Besides, I don't need to drink in the same way my mother did. I have a glass of wine now and again for pleasure, not because I need it.'

There were six bottles in total but two were empty. One because the cork had shrunk and the wine had leaked out, and the other because the bottle had broken. The nest was also empty — probably because the baby mice had grown old enough to run away. Finn handed Hope another bottle.

'These look really ancient.' she remarked. 'I can't read the label, but I doubt any of this is fit to drink.'

'We'll take the bottles upstairs,

anyway,' she said. 'They go with the house — a little bit of nostalgia. We can display them in the restaurant.'

Suddenly Finn sniffed and swung his torch around the cellar. 'Can you smell smoke?'

Hope blinked, realising her eyes had been smarting for several minutes. Finn shone his torch towards the cellar door — and she saw a curl of smoke in the beam. Quickly she stood the two bottles back on the shelf and looked at him worriedly.

'It's coming from upstairs.'

He ran up the stairs, bursting into the kitchen. Smoke filled the room, making him cough. Hope was right behind him. The smoke caught in her throat, making her eyes water.

'What is it? Where's it coming from?' She remembered they had left the door open into the garden. Now it was shut.

The metal bin Finn used for rubbish stood in the middle of the floor, gushing clouds of smoke. Calling to her to open the door, Finn picked up the bin, cursing when the hot meal burned his hands, and rushed outside with it, setting it down on the flagstones.

As he came back inside, Hope handed him a piece of paper. 'I found this on the table.'

The message was brief, printed with a soft pencil on a scrap of paper torn from a spiral bound notebook. *This was just a warning.*

Finn looked at her, his face grim. 'Todd?'

She shook her head, bewildered. 'Surely not. What would be the point?'

'To scare me away from you — or burn my house down. This place would go up like a tinderbox, and I don't have insurance, I can't afford it.'

'You've got enough problems,' she said angrily. 'You don't need this.' She looked round the kitchen. 'He's been in here, hasn't he? I left the back door open. He must have come in while we were in the cellar and set light to the bin. I'm so sorry, Finn.'

He pulled her into his arms. 'It's not

your fault, and no harm's been done. He'll soon realise I don't give up easily. Tell me where he lives.' He gave her a little shake. 'Let me sort this out, Hope.'

'No, I'll speak to him. It's my problem, not yours.'

She couldn't let Finn suffer because of her, she thought.

'If you think he might have done this, stay away from him. I don't want you to get hurt.'

She didn't cry on the way home. She felt numb. Finn had tried to make her stay, but she had pleaded tiredness and a sore throat from the smoke. She was still finding it difficult to believe Todd had behaved in this way. It was a side of him she had never seen before. He was stubborn and bigoted and small-minded, but she had never known him to be this vindictive.

She would have expected him to either confront Finn head-on, or convince himself the whole marriage thing had been a bad idea, and give up.

She glanced at the dashboard clock. Just coming up to five-thirty. If Todd had been responsible for the fire and the note, he should be back home by now. She turned left at the traffic lights and headed for the river. If she could talk to Todd, she might be able to make him see how silly he was being and, whatever he did, nothing was going to make her change her mind.

Noticing his car in the car park, she used the code he had given her to gain entry to the apartment building. Security was paramount here, and even the lift needed a separate code. She made her way along the carpeted corridor and rang the bell outside his door.

Opening it, he gave her a cool smile. 'Changed your mind already? That was impressively quick.'

'I'm sorry, Todd, I really am,' she said quickly. 'I know I hurt your feelings and made you feel stupid — but you can't burn Finn's house down just to get back at me.'

He blinked. 'I don't know what

131

you're talking about, Hope.'

She could feel the anger and frustration building up inside her. 'Listen to me,' she said furiously. 'I'm going to stay with Finn whatever happens, and if you threaten him any more I'm going to the police. I won't let you destroy his house.'

Todd frowned. 'Someone threatened Finn Masters?'

'Are you telling me you didn't set light to the bin in Finn's kitchen?'

'I'm telling you exactly that. I have no idea what you're talking about.'

He might not have done the deed himself, but Hope was sure he knew who had. She had seen a look of recognition come into his eyes when she mentioned the burning rubbish bin.

The house burning down would solve the builder's problems. They didn't want to buy the house; they just wanted the land.

'You're working with the developers, aren't you, Todd? Did you put up the money? Is that what you're worried about? If Finn doesn't sell you'll be one of the people losing out, won't you?'

Before he could reply, she turned her back on him and hurried to the emergency stairs. If she waited for the lift he might come after her, and right now she couldn't bear to look at him.

By the time she got home it was dark, and once she had washed the smell of smoke out of her hair and made herself a sandwich, she was exhausted. She went to bed early, and dreamed of a mouse the size of a dragon and a dragon slayer with a mousetrap instead of a sword.

8

On Sunday morning, once again the ringing of the phone pulled Hope out of a deep sleep. For a moment she thought she was late for work. She looked at her bedside clock. Only one person would wake her at the crack of dawn on a Sunday.

When she picked up the phone, Finn said, 'Can you come over?'

She could — but she didn't know whether she should. It was a wonder he wanted to see her again. Before he could change his mind, she said, 'When do you want me?'

His chuckle made her smile. She had forgotten how good it sounded.

'Right now, if you can manage it. You sound all sleepy and delicious. Are you still in bed?'

She decided not to answer to that question as it might get her into even more trouble. 'I'll be with you in about half an hour. Do you have anything for breakfast?'

He told her he did, so she quickly showered and pulled on jeans and a thin jumper. The weather had changed overnight, as it does, and the day outside looked grey and rather chilly.

She wanted to see Finn so much, she had to take her foot off the accelerator several times or she would have exceeded the speed limit. She was pleased to see that the only car in the driveway belonged to Finn.

He met her at the kitchen door and caught her up in his arms.

'I missed you.'

'I've only been gone for a few hours. That was all the sleep you allowed me.' She looked around the clean and tidy kitchen. 'No more fires, then?'

His smile didn't quite reach his eyes. 'I'll tell you later, after breakfast.'

She looked at him worriedly, but the smell of food made her realise how hungry she was. He was right. Breakfast came first; any problems could be dealt with later.

She made coffee and set the table while he fried bacon and toasted bread, leaving her to scramble some eggs.

'I got up at the crack of dawn to shop,' he said. 'So we have fresh orange juice and cream for the coffee.'

'A special occasion?'

'Not really. I just wanted to apologise for maligning your boyfriend. Sorry, ex-boyfriend. He wasn't the one who lit the fire.'

Hope nodded. 'I found that out as well. Do you know who did?'

'Someone employed by the builder, I think. They stand to lose so much money if I don't agree to sell, they're prepared to go to almost any lengths to force my hand. I got a phone call yesterday evening reminding me the house wasn't covered by fire insurance and likely to burn down if anyone accidentally dropped a match. The caller finished off by saying there was no smoke without fire. Not particularly original, but quite good as a threat.'

'Have you called the police?'

'A phone call isn't evidence, Hope. And the note could have been written by anybody.'

Before she had time to answer, he took her by the shoulders and gently pushed her into a chair. 'Stop asking questions and sit down and eat your breakfast. I don't want to talk with my mouth full.'

She did as she was told, enjoying the taste of the salty bacon with the buttery eggs and crisp toast. She was dying to ask Finn more questions but waited until they both had a steaming cup of coffee in front of them.

'What are you going to do?'

'Nothing. There's nothing I can do at the moment. If I can get a bank loan to do the improvements and cover the cost of the tax on the house, I can tell the builders to get lost, but until then I need to keep my options open. If I have to sell the house, theirs is the best offer

I'm going to get. Probably the only offer.'

She looked at him in dismay. They had done so much work already. He had found a company that sold heritage paints, and the walls in the main room were now pale terracotta; the floor had been sanded and sealed, and the woodwork was clean and bright. Her work on the kitchen floor had given the tiles back their original glow and you could actually see out of the windows. The thought of it all being pulled down made her feel sick.

'The bank will give you the money, I know they will.' She paused as she collected the plates and mugs. 'Todd may not have lit the fire, but he's mixed up in this. I'd hate to see him win.'

While she was helping him wash up the breakfast dishes, she noticed he had brought the old wine bottles up from the basement. They now had pride of place on the dresser.

'How did you get the bottles clean?' she asked.

'With difficulty. I was going to throw the wine out and wash the bottles properly, but I couldn't get the corks out without breaking them and I didn't want the labels to come off, so I just wiped them down. They look good, don't they? Really authentic.'

'Because they are authentic. Except one of them isn't a bottle of wine, it's a bottle of whisky. I wonder if it's still drinkable? Spirit keeps, doesn't it?'

Finn picked up the bottle. 'It was bottled in 1926, so it's pretty old. I reckon Grandad hid it from my grandmother so she wouldn't tip it down the sink. She hated him drinking.'

'So that means you mustn't ever drink it, either,' Hope said decisively, taking the bottle away from him. 'We'll keep it unopened in her memory.'

'Will you come round on Monday evening?' Finn asked. 'I have an appointment with the bank in the afternoon. I don't suppose I'll be very long.' He gave her a rueful smile. 'But I might need you here to console me when I get back.'

'Of course I'll come — but to help you celebrate.'

* * *

Once they had cleared up, Finn went outside to do some heavy work in the garden. He had found some old paving slabs stacked in a comer and he was hoping there would be enough to extend the patio.

Hope wandered round the house humming to herself, thinking she might bring a radio next time she came. Music while they worked would be nice. They had painted the walls of the bedroom Finn was using, just to make it look clean and tidy, and the bathroom was beginning to take shape. The bath would have to be re-enamelled, but the porcelain basin and toilet now gleamed. It had been Finn's idea to give the floorboards a wash of white paint, and Hope had found a handmade rug in an art shop that kept the splinters out of bare feet.

She was standing in the big room downstairs, wondering what colour drapes they should choose for the windows, when she heard a thumping on the front door.

It was obviously not Finn — he would have come in round the back. She hesitated, wondering if she should open the door. If it was Todd, she could cope, but if it was one of the builders she might be in serious trouble. Finn was nowhere in sight, and for the first time she realised how isolated the house was.

The first thing she saw when she opened the door was Todd's Mercedes parked on the drive.

Todd scowled at her. 'Where is he?'

'Todd, what are you doing here?'

'I came to see the opposition.' He gave a short bark of a laugh and looked round the hallway disparagingly. 'For goodness' sake, Hope, what is wrong with you?'

She stepped back. He looked really angry.

'Finn's working in the garden, Todd.'

'So?' He moved past her, turned into the big room and seemed to calm down. 'Getting the house ready for resale, is he? He'll be lucky. The house isn't worth diddly squat, however much he tarts it up.'

'What do you want, Todd?'

'Tell your boyfriend to take the builder's offer, it's the best he's going to get. Much better to pull the house down and let a bunch of builders worry about planning applications and stuff like that.' He strolled through to the kitchen. 'So this is why you left me? Property is money, and boyfriend number two is all set to become a millionaire. A clever move on your part. My mother was right. You're nothing but a little gold-digger, Hope.'

When she ignored him, he turned to leave. 'Give my regards to your boyfriend and tell him he's welcome. I'm sure you'll stay with him until something better comes along.'

'Hope? What's happening?'

She turned as Finn came in through the back door. His jeans were muddy and his hair was standing on end where he must have run his hands through it, but to her he looked wonderful.

Todd, immaculate in his pale grey business suit, his tie perfectly knotted, put down his briefcase and held out a hand, but Finn ignored it.

'Do I know you?'

'Todd Bartlett. Hope's fiancé.'

Finn raised a lazy eyebrow. 'No, I don't think you are. Not any more. She was engaged to you but now she's with me, so I'd like you to leave my house without causing any trouble.'

Normally Todd didn't lose his temper — he believed in negotiation — but Hope watched the blood rush to his face and settle in angry red blotches.

'Trouble?' He waved an arm in Hope's direction. 'She's the one causing trouble. Accusing me of setting your house on fire and goodness knows what else. You don't know what you're taking on, Masters. She's unhinged. She's having a nervous breakdown or something. My mother always said she wasn't quite right in the head.'

'I asked you to leave, Todd,' Finn said quietly. 'I don't want to have to call the police, but I will. Hope told you she didn't want to see you again, so this is tantamount to stalking.' Keeping his eyes on Todd, he picked up the other man's briefcase and held it out. 'Want me to show you the way out?'

Hope's eyes darted from one man to the other. They were about the same height, but there the similarity ended. Finn was lean and well muscled, and exuded a sense of menace that Todd couldn't match. She knew which one her money would be on, but she didn't want them to come to blows.

'Please,' she said, holding up her hand to keep them apart. 'Please leave, Todd. I don't want you to fight over me.'

'This isn't about you, Hope.' Finn's

eyes were as cold as the North Sea. 'I asked this gentleman to leave my house, and I'm still waiting for him to do so. He's trespassing, and if he won't leave of his own accord I'm going to call the police.'

Finn picked up the phone. Todd clearly couldn't take any more. He grabbed a bottle from the dresser and rounded on Finn, holding the bottle with both hands like a baseball bat.

'Don't push your luck with me, mate.' His accent had reverted to pure Essex. 'I was going to leave anyway, but I'm fed up with being pushed around by a layabout like you. I don't suppose you ever worked a day in your life, did you? Just sat back and waited for Granny to drop dead so you could inherit her house. I've had to work for what I've got.'

Still wielding the bottle, he glared at Hope. 'And she thinks she can string me along and then dump me whenever she pleases.'

'Oh, for goodness' sake.' Finn sat

down and kicked off his shoes. 'If you want to be a drama queen, you'll have to do it on your own. I'm tired.'

Todd had been made to look a fool yet again, and it was all too much for him. With no escape for his pent-up anger, he raised the bottle above his head, about to hit Finn. Before Finn could move, Hope launched herself at Todd with a shriek, punching him in the stomach.

Todd was so surprised by her sudden attack that he let go of the bottle, but Finn reached out from his chair and caught it one-handed before it hit the floor. A catch that would have made a first-class cricketer proud.

Hope took the bottle from him and stood it back on the dresser, her heart pounding so fast she thought she was going to faint, but when both men looked at her in amazement, she managed a little shrug.

'I hate clearing up broken glass.'

Todd turned his back and left quietly without another word.

* * *

Hope left work promptly on Monday so she could reach the house before Finn got back from the bank. As she walked round the side of the building, she was surprised to see the kitchen door open. She would have expected Finn to lock up securely after the fire in the bin so she slowed her pace, poking her head gingerly round the kitchen door.

An elderly man was sitting at the kitchen table and when their eyes met he gave her a big smile. He didn't really look as if he could do much harm, but Hope had been so surprised to see him sitting there that she barely stifled a scream.

The man scrambled hastily to his feet. 'You must be Hope. Sorry if I startled you.'

She walked further into the kitchen, not sure whether to be reassured that he knew her name, or even more frightened.

'Excuse me, but who are you?'

'Travis.' He held out his hand. 'Travis Masters. Finn's uncle.'

Uncle? Finn had never mentioned any living relatives. 'Finn had a bank appointment,' she said warily.

'I know. I arrived before he left. Looked right smart, he did.' Travis pulled out a chair. 'Sit yourself down and I'll make you a mug of coffee. Finn told me all about you.' The smile was back. 'Didn't do you justice, though.'

'I'm pleased to meet you, Travis,' she told him, reassured at last. 'I didn't know Finn had an uncle.'

The man's hair was bushy and already starting to go white, and wire-framed glasses rested low down on his nose giving him a scholarly appearance. *The archetypal mad professor*, she thought, as she held out her hand. To her surprise, Travis bent his head and kissed the tips of her fingers.

At that moment Finn walked in by the back door. Hope had only ever seen him casually dressed, but now he wore a dark suit that fitted his broad shoulders perfectly. He was carrying a leather briefcase, and she thought he looked like a younger version of James Bond.

'Wonderful, Finn!' Travis said exuberantly. 'You've waited a long time, but, by golly, it was worth it! Where have you been hiding her?'

Finn laughed. 'Sit down, Hope, and have some coffee. You can ignore Travis, he's as mad as a hatter.'

She sat down while Travis fetched clean mugs from the dresser. They both looked at Finn.

'What happened, then?' Hope asked. 'What did the bank say? Are they going to give you a loan?'

He dropped in to a chair beside her. 'Yes.' When she looked as if she was about to cheer, he held up his hand. 'But with conditions. They want me to put up forty thousand pounds myself. Much more than I've got. I don't think we can do this, Hope — it's going to be really tight and we can only economise so much.'

Travis spoke. 'I've always looked out for you, boy, haven't I? And if you want money, you know you only have to ask. Tell you what — let me be a partner in this enterprise. You'd be doing me a favour. The house is a wonderful setting for a restaurant, and the bank must have thought so as well or they wouldn't have agreed to lend you money.'

When Hope looked at him, Finn shook his head. 'Don't worry, we've already been through this. I need to do this myself, Uncle Travis. Hope is the only partner I want — it has to be our project. Maybe we'll take on a partner some time in the future, but not right now.'

Travis turned to Hope. 'Stubborn little blighter, isn't he? Always was, if I remember rightly.'

He stood up and walked over to the dresser. 'I had a look at these bottles while you were out. Where did you get them?'

'They were hidden in a corner of the

cellar. I thought they'd make a good display in the restaurant. A bit of nostalgia.'

Travis picked up the bottle of whisky and stared at the label. 'You got a laptop, Finn?'

Finn undid his briefcase. 'Of course I have. Why?'

'Macallan whisky. Look it up on the internet. I've come across that name before somewhere.'

Finn put his laptop on the table beside the bottle. 'Travis is an antique dealer. He bought a lot of Grandma's stuff before the sale and gave me a good price for it. Probably too much.'

He had been punching keys, and now he looked up with a strange expression on his face. 'A bottle of 1926 Macallan Fine and Rare whisky sold in America for thirty-eight thousand dollars, and it's rumoured that it was then sold on to a Japanese buyer for a lot more.'

Travis punched the air. 'I remember now! Everyone thought that was the last bottle that was going to surface. There aren't any more around.'

Hope picked up the bottle very carefully and put it back on the dresser. 'That was the bottle Todd tried to break over your head.'

'If he'd succeeded, I'd have had a very expensive concussion.'

Travis picked up a wine bottle. 'These might be worth something, too.' He turned to Finn. 'Sell me the lot, Finn, for forty thousand. That'll give you the money you need for the bank, and you can get a talking fish or something to put in the restaurant. I'll be taking a risk — but so will you.'

Finn looked stunned. 'How will I be taking a risk?'

Travis gave a wolfish grin. 'Because if they fetch double that amount, I'll be ripping you off something rotten.'

'We can't let you do that,' Hope said. 'What if the bottles are worthless?'

'I'm a gambler, Hope. This is not an altruistic offer. I'll do all the work, but I expect to make a nice profit.'

'You put them up for auction,' Finn

said, 'and we'll share any profit fifty-fifty. That seems a lot fairer.'

Travis shook his head. 'No. I don't share anything, Finn. You should know that. Sell them to me, or auction them yourselves.'

Finn looked at Hope. 'What shall we do?'

'It seems like a good offer to me. Your uncle is taking a gamble, but if that one bottle of whisky finds a Japanese buyer, you're the one out of pocket, not him.'

Travis grinned and held out his hand. 'She's got a head on her shoulders, that one. Shake on it, boy, and I'll transfer the money straight into your bank account tomorrow.'

Finn shook his uncle's hand. 'Thank you. I really hope you make a lot of money. Tell you what — with my newfound fortune, I'll treat you both to lunch at the pub.'

9

By the end of the week, Finn was exhausted. Now he had the promise of the bank loan and had paid off all the bills, he was looking forward getting on with work on the house, but he was snowed under with paperwork and none of the major alterations could go ahead until planning permission had been passed, which would take weeks.

His friend had checked the files at the Town Hall and told him there was another application pending — for total demolition of the house and a proposal for building more than twenty four-bedroom detached houses, and one five-bedroom house with a swimming pool.

The house Todd had intended building for Hope.

Finn phoned the planning office and patiently explained that he was the rightful owner of the land and had no intention of selling any of it. He could almost sense the shrug on the other end of the line.

'Very well, sir, we'll do what we can to process your application as quickly as possible, but it's for a change of usage, isn't it? They take time.'

Finn agreed that it was. Nothing was ever straightforward. He glanced at the daily paper lying on the coffee table and was surprised to see it was already Friday. Where had the week gone? If the rest of the days flew past as quickly as this, it would be no time at all before they could get the interior work started.

Having met Todd in person, he realised the man wasn't at all what he had expected. Todd was tall and good-looking, he dressed impeccably, and he probably loved Hope — to the best of his ability, anyway. Finn was beginning to wonder if he was being totally selfish in trying to keep Hope for himself.

When she arrived that evening, he

suggested they send out for pizza, and the same teenager delivered it as before. This time, though, he waited long enough for Finn to give him a tip.

'Place looks nice,' the boy said. 'Brighter.' Then he pocketed his money and cycled happily away.

Finn laughed. 'See? The house is no longer haunted. We've driven away the ghosts.'

Hope chose a slice of pizza and looked at him with shining eyes. 'No, your grand-mother's ghost is still around, but now she's a happy ghost.'

He wanted to take Hope in his arms and kiss her, pizza and all. She never failed to amaze him, and he couldn't believe she had chosen him over a millionaire, even if the millionaire was a complete idiot. Her hair was catching the last of the evening sunlight and shimmered with gold highlights that matched the amber of her eyes. She was the most beautiful thing he had ever seen.

She suggested they make the most of

the balmy evening, and they were sitting on the patio outside the kitchen door, drinking chilled white wine, when Finn heard the letterbox slam shut.

He put down his wine glass. 'What the devil was that? I never get junk mail.' He went back into the kitchen, puzzled by the strange whooshing sound coming from the hall. Opening the door without thinking, he was faced with a wall of flame.

He leapt back, slamming the door shut to stop Hope going any further. 'Fill the sink with water as quickly as you can, but don't open the door.'

He grabbed a dust sheet they had been using to stop paint getting on the kitchen tiles and dropped it into the sink, turning on the tap, then he ran into the big room and grabbed another one.

'We can't throw water on the flames. That's burning petrol out there and water will just spread the fire. We're going to have to try and smother it. I'll go round the other way.'

While Hope soaked the second sheet, he dropped the first sheet into the mop bucket and ran through the main room, reaching the hall from a different direction. Hope followed him with the second sheet trailing on the floor. The fire was at its worst near the front door. The petrol had formed pools on the floor and rivers of flame were creeping along the mosaic tiles. The skirting boards were black and blistered where the flames had touched them, but the wood was thick and it would take a while to catch fire.

He flung his sheet over the flames and ran on to it, stamping his feet. Hope passed him the second sheet and he threw it over the remaining pool of burning liquid, then he ran back into the kitchen and filled the bucket with water, tipping it over the sheets already on the floor. Between them they eventually managed to put out the flames.

As Hope gazed at the charred

skirting and blackened walls in consternation, Finn put an arm round her shoulders.

'I don't think we can blame Todd for this one. I heard a motorbike screaming away as I opened the door into the hall.'

She laughed shakily. 'You shut it again pretty quickly, didn't you!'

A quick assessment of the damage showed it was limited to the hallway. A couple of the doors, including the front door, were badly scorched, but the hard old wood wasn't easy to set alight.

'Whoever it was didn't know the floor was tiled. If the floor had been wood planks, like the rest of the house, the petrol would have soaked in and the whole damned place would have burned down. As it was, the petrol just pooled on the tiles and they can be cleaned and repaired.'

He walked back into the kitchen and picked up the phone. 'But this time, we call the police.'

They came quickly — a detective in plain clothes, who introduced himself as Detective Constable Martin, and a woman in uniform. Finn produced the letter from the builders and the threatening note, and got told off for not reporting the previous incident.

'If you'd contacted us the first time, we might have been able to prevent this happening,' DC Martin said.

The fire had been caused, he continued, by something filled with petrol being pushed through the letterbox. 'Could have been anything. Probably a plastic bag dropped through the letterbox like a water bomb, followed by a lighted match — that would do the trick. Whatever they used got burned up.'

The policeman took out his phone and called for a fingerprint expert.

'There's a beauty on the letterbox,' he told them. 'You can see it with the naked eye. He was an amateur. He didn't bother to wear gloves because he wasn't coming inside the house, so what does he do? Pushes up the letterbox flap with his bare thumb. Like I said, an amateur.'

Finn and Hope were told not to touch anything in the hall or outside the front door until someone from the forensic department had been out to see them, probably in the morning.

Hope wanted to clean the tiles and wash down the walls straight away, and Finn could understand why. He hated seeing the beautiful inlaid pattern on the floor smothered with ash and water. It seemed every bit of good luck was countered by something bad happening, and he was beginning to wonder if their project was cursed.

Hope was tired and thoroughly shaken, and Finn suggested she stay the night. He offered to sleep on the floor and let her have his bed, and promised he wouldn't take advantage of her, but she said she needed to go home. It was almost dark, and she wanted to get away while there was still some light in the sky.

He walked with her round the back of the house to her car, and she clung to him for longer than usual. 'Why would someone do that? We could both have been burned to death.'

'But we weren't. The police will pick up the person who did this. Everything will be fine, Hope, believe me. There are always problems of some sort, and if you want something badly enough, you just have to ride them out. Tomorrow is another day.'

He wished he had persuaded her to stay, and thought of camping outside her house in his car just to make sure she was safe. But it wasn't Hope they were after — it was the house. If the house burned down, he would have nothing left. He would be homeless and destitute.

He kissed her goodbye. 'You'll see. Everything will be just fine.'

Fighting the urge to clean up the hall, he stepped over the wet sheets and went upstairs to his bedroom, thinking ruefully that he would probably sleep much better if Hope had been beside him.

Hope climbed in to her car and drove home to her little cottage. After the trauma of the last few hours, it felt like a sanctuary.

She didn't sleep well. The night had turned sultry, an oppressive heat that probably heralded a storm, and she woke several times thinking her house was on fire. She had just fallen into a deep sleep when her alarm went off, and she was glad she had set it the night before. She needed to be with Finn when the fingerprint man arrived.

She was pleased she had decided to clean the brass door fittings. The letterbox had been buffed up to a mirror-like shine, the perfect place to catch a fingerprint.

She picked up a bag of doughnuts on the way, in case Finn had forgotten to stock up with items for breakfast. Because of his shift work he often forgot what day of the week it was, and he knew he could always get something to eat when he arrived at the Country Club.

They had beans on toast, which was about all Finn had left on the shelves of the old-fashioned larder, followed by doughnuts and coffee, which Hope decided was a truly superb breakfast by any standard.

They had just cleared the table when Detective Constable Martin walked in through the back door, followed by a man with a black canvas bag.

'We've already taken the fingerprint from the letterbox and picked up a good shoe print as well,' Martin said. 'If the silly idiot had kept to the path he would have been all right, but he was in such a hurry he cut across the flower bed and left a footprint in all that nicely raked soil.'

Hope smiled at Finn. 'My beautifully polished letterbox and your nice smooth flower bed. We make a good team for collecting evidence.'

'I'm sure his fingerprints will be on file,' Martin said. 'He's such an idiot he's bound to have been caught before. The shoe print is just an extra nail in his coffin. Those builders have already got themselves a reputation round here. If people don't want to move, they get intimidated until they sell below list price. One old lady living on her own had a heart attack when they popped a rat through her letterbox.'

'We've got some of those.' Hope shuddered. 'We don't need any more.'

'Mice,' Finn corrected. 'They were field mice, and anyway if it hadn't been for the mice we'd never have found . . . '

'Okay, we probably owe them, but we could've killed them and we didn't. Instead, we found them a new home.'

Travis turned up just as the police were leaving. Finn filled him in about the fire and DC Martin gave him a funny look, but the policeman didn't ask Travis any questions. The old man didn't look much like an arsonist.

'I came to tell you I've got a date for the auction and I've come to pick up my bottles. Thank goodness you didn't wash the labels off, Finn. The bottles would have been worthless.'

'Not for want of trying,' Finn said. 'I'm sure the wine is corked, but that doesn't matter, does it?'

Travis shook his head. 'No one in their right mind is going to try and drink the stuff in those bottles. Even if the wine was still drinkable, once you open the bottle, it loses its value.' He held the Macallan up to the light. 'Mind you, a glass of whisky right now would go down a treat . . .'

Hope grabbed the bottle. 'Can we take him to the pub for lunch and get him a drink? I worry about him being near that bottle. We should probably lock it in a safe somewhere.'

'That's a good idea,' Travis said. 'I'd rather leave the bottles here until I've got a date for the auction, but this place is hardly burglar-proof and, right now, we're all going to be up at the pub.'

'We could put them back where we found them for now,' Finn suggested.

'The mice kept them safe for a long time and even if someone broke in, the cellar looks empty.'

They carried the bottles carefully down to the cellar and put them back on the ledge. The mice had gone, and in a way Hope missed them. She hoped they were happy in their new home.

★ ★ ★

Over lunch they told Travis about their plans for the restaurant.

'You need to get estimates straight away for the work you can't do yourselves,' he told Finn, 'and don't take on more than you can manage. You're used to sleek, modern hotel décor, and that house needs something completely different.'

'We know that,' Hope said. 'You saw what we've already done to the upstairs. That's how we want to keep it. As authentic as possible. The plumbing will be modern because no one will see it, but the bathroom fittings are all original and the china basins are still beautiful. We'll need a lot of furniture for downstairs — the Victorians used to stuff their houses full of bits and pieces — but we can get all that second-hand from junk stalls and car boot sales. You'd be surprised what people throw out.'

Finn ordered more beer. Talking was thirsty work. 'It's a pity I had to sell all Grandma's things.'

'Most of your grandmother's furniture was too modern.' Hope smiled at Finn's look of surprise. 'You said your grandmother was eighty-three when she died, so she missed both the Victorian and Edwardian periods. In fact, she must have been born about the time that precious Macallan whisky was bottled. Perhaps that's why your grandfather kept it so long,' she offered.

Finn looked worried. 'Perhaps I shouldn't sell it.'

Travis laughed in disbelief. 'She wanted you to keep the house, Finn, not a bottle of whisky she hated, and you never knew your grandfather, so you don't owe him anything.'

Finn picked up his beer with a sigh of relief. 'Thank goodness for that. This inheritance thing was beginning to look even more complicated.'

10

The next few weeks passed so quickly, Hope wondered where they had gone. With the bank loan agreed and the inheritance tax paid at last, she felt they had been given a breathing space. The police had already picked up the man who tried to set light to the house and managed to connect him to the builders, who were now being prosecuted. The court case would go on for ages, but the builders weren't likely to cause any more problems while they were under close police scrutiny.

Hope couldn't afford the mortgage on her house unless she worked, but she hated her office job, so she found part-time work at a little boutique in town and loved every minute of it. The money was half the amount she had been getting for working at the council, but the other two girls who worked in the shop were really nice — someone to chat with about girly things and share lunch with in the back room of the shop. Apart from that, the shorter hours meant she could spend more time at the house.

They finished the painting and studied swatches and colour charts until their eyes ached — but Finn hadn't kissed her since Travis left, and seemed determined to keep their relationship on a purely businesslike level.

She was beginning to fear he had gone off her, and couldn't imagine why. He was always friendly, and sometimes she saw him watching her with what could only be described as a hungry look, but he didn't make a move and she wasn't going to push him. She had made a terrible mistake with Todd and she didn't intend doing the same thing again. She shook herself. If Finn wanted to be cool and distant, he could jolly well get on with it.

The auction was due in a couple of

days and she knew Finn was worrying about the bottles turning out to be worthless. Travis had returned with a special crate and the bottles had been removed from the cellar and sent to London, where they were now awaiting their fate.

The evening before the sale, a mouse appeared in the kitchen and her squeak had Finn rushing into the room.

'It was a mouse,' she said.

He gave her a disbelieving look. 'A mouse didn't make that noise.'

'No, that was me, because I saw a mouse run under the cellar door. They're back, Finn.'

'I don't think so. It would have been a hell of a long walk home.'

Annoyed because he didn't believe her, she threw open the cellar door and started down the stairs, completely forgetting there was no light. Her foot caught on a broken step halfway down and she tumbled to the bottom, finishing up in a heap on the dirty floor. Finn came charging down behind her, calling her name, but she was still cross with him. It was his fault she had fallen down the steps, and he had no right ignoring her for weeks and then suddenly pretending he cared.

He knelt down beside her and gathered her into his arms. 'Are you hurt? Speak to me, Hope. Please tell me you're all right.'

She realised he couldn't tell whether her eyes were open or shut in the dark, and decided to take advantage of the situation. If it hadn't been for him, she wouldn't have fallen in the first place. He deserved to suffer a little.

She moaned softly, wondering how someone would sound if every bone in their body was broken. Concussion — that was a good one, easy to fake. She gave another groan and heard him make a noise that sounded suspiciously like a sob. Perhaps he really did care.

'Please speak to me, Hope. I love you so much.' He brushed the hair away from her face and kissed her gently. 'I've got to leave you, my darling, I've have to go and call an ambulance.'

Leave her? In the dark with the mice? No way! She sat up quickly, and gave a real groan. Every bone in her body seemed to be protesting, but she wriggled her fingers and toes and decided nothing was actually broken. 'What did you say, Finn?'

He kissed her again. 'I'll have to leave you for a moment to go upstairs and call an ambulance.'

'No, before that.' She slid both arms round his neck. 'Something about loving me.'

He peered at her face in the darkness. 'Were you faking?'

'There is no way I could fake a fall like that, but I don't think I'm going to die. Not just yet, anyway.' She snuggled further into his lap. 'I'm sure I heard you say you loved me. Or was concussion making me hear things?'

He removed her arms from around his neck and helped her to her feet. 'I don't think you've got concussion, and I would offer to carry you up the stairs, but I'd probably drop you, so you'll have to hang on to me and hobble. We'll decide whether you need an ambulance when I can look at you in the light.'

He sat her on a kitchen chair and examined every bit of her he could see. The bits he couldn't see would have to wait. She had a graze on her elbow and a cut on her hand where she had landed on the hard floor, and enough bruises to darken her skin in a number of places, but otherwise she felt pretty good. Her ankle was slightly puffy, and she knew she had a big bruise on her bottom that was going to be painful for a few days, but she kept that bit of information to herself.

'No ambulance, then,' Finn said, adding severely, 'but you deserve a good spanking for scaring me like that, my girl.'

Never mind that — he still hadn't answered her question.

'Finn, you said you loved me. Did you mean it? You've hardly spoken to me for days and I thought you didn't want me around any more.'

'Of course I want you around. Unfortunately, I don't think I can live without you, but I worked out the figures and I'm going to be completely broke. Not only broke, but in debt up to my eyebrows.'

He slipped off her shoe and took her foot on his lap, gently feeling around her ankle. 'Todd was well off. He had a job with a pension, a flat in the best part of town, a Mercedes . . . the list just goes on. The restaurant will take months to get off the ground and I'm going to have to give up my job at the Country Club to oversee all the alterations.'

He sighed. 'I want my own business, Hope, but I've been incredibly selfish. I've already cost you your job and your marriage. I can't ask for anything more.'

'You could ask me to marry you.' What? She didn't know where that had come from. It had just sort of popped out.

He looked at her strangely. 'You said you didn't want to get married for years. You said you liked being free and independent — your own person.'

Had she really said all that? She must have thought she meant it at the time — but now, with Finn kneeling at her feet, his hand gently stroking her ankle, she was thinking about something else altogether.

His fingers caught a painful spot and she yelped. 'Ouch, that hurt.'

'Sorry, I wasn't concentrating. Did you just ask me to marry you?'

'No.' She shook her head. 'I suggested you ask me, which is more conventional — but as you just pointed out you're not much of a catch, I might say no if you did.'

'That would definitely be the sensible thing to do. I don't have a big diamond ring to give you, but I do have a beautiful house and more love than you could ever imagine.' He leaned forward and gently kissed her lips. 'And if I promise to do all the cooking, would that be enough to tempt you?'

'It might.' She slid her arms round his neck. 'Try me.'

'I'm already on my knees on a hard kitchen floor, and you know I love you, Hope Brown, so will you marry me?'

She laughed with happiness. 'Yes, please.'

She wanted to tell everyone, but all her friends thought she was still engaged to Todd, so it might be a bit of a shock to find out she was going to marry someone else.

'Let's have a party!' she declared, gesturing for Finn to help her up. She hobbled over to the fridge. 'Have you got any wine?'

Finn grabbed a couple of glasses. 'I've got wine, but there's only you and me. Is that enough for a party?'

She giggled. 'Actually, I didn't mean right now, but a glass of wine would be nice. I meant a party to celebrate our engagement and publicise the restaurant at the same time. The big room looks great now we've painted it, and we could get trestle tables and you could make some canapé things. We could invite the whole village!' She stopped talking abruptly for several moments while he kissed her appreciatively, and then once she had caught her breath, took a sip of the wine he handed her. 'What do you think?'

'I think you're wonderful, Hope Brown. A village party would be perfect. We can invite the local press and get a write-up in the paper. Maybe even a local television interview.'

But she was shaking her head. 'That's not what we want, is it, Finn? We planned a place where people could bring their kids and have a nice lunch or an evening meal without getting stressed out. If we publicise the place too much, we'll get the jumped-up middle classes queuing for a table, particularly as you're an international chef — but if we say the kids will be taken care of because they'll have their own supervised play area, that'll bring in the mums and dads, and they'll tell everyone else.'

'And I do make the best double-fried chips in the whole world.'

'False modesty has never been one of your failings, has it, Finn? Come on, we've got lots of work to do.'

★ ★ ★

It took another month to get the party organised, and by then Travis had phoned to say he had made a nice profit at the auction. Finn asked the landlord from the village pub to help with the catering, and also roped in a couple of friends from the Country Club. Travis came to stay and arranged for the hire of tables and chairs for the big day, and Hope took over the computer and printed off enough invitations for the whole village.

They were lucky with the weather. The first week in October gave them an Indian summer with temperatures in the seventies, and Finn was able to open the doors on to the terrace. He had pinned a big drawing of the proposed plans on the wall so everyone could see how the place would look in a few months' time. He was hoping to open the restaurant early in the New Year.

Hope hardly slept the night before the party. She arrived at the house in the early light, to find Finn and Travis already hard at work. The sanded and polished floor of the big room positively glowed with its fresh coating of wax, the tables had been covered with long white cloths, and Hope had picked flowers from the garden to add scent and colour to the room. Most of the food was to be served cold and already sitting in the fridge, but Finn was determined to serve bowls of his famous chips with home-made tomato sauce.

People started arriving early, hoping for a tour of the house. Hope was determined to retain some privacy, however, so she made sure the visitors were restricted to the ground floor.

Finn had persuaded the local garden centre to loan him patio sets, complete with price tags, but when the furniture arrived they found the manager had also included a dozen wooden tubs filled with brilliantly coloured flowers, all with their prices prominently displayed. Hope dotted them around the terrace. All good advertising for the garden centre.

She flitted from table to table, thoroughly enjoying herself — until she spotted Todd with a pretty little blonde on his arm. He was swaggering around the room with a sneer on his face, obviously intent on disliking everything he saw.

He picked up a prawn canapé, sniffed it, and then put it back on the plate. Hope felt like running across the room and slapping his hand.

'Who invited him?' she hissed to Finn. 'He doesn't live in the village.'

Finn excused himself from the old lady he had been talking to and moved to the side of the room with Hope. 'I've noticed one or two of the Country Club crowd here, and I know we didn't invite them.'

She looked around anxiously, biting her lip. 'Do you think Todd is going to cause trouble?'

'He can try, but I don't think he'll get very far.'

The room was full of happy, smiling people, mostly families from the village. Hope had managed to rig up a temporary play area with a plastic slide and swing for the little ones, and the older children were chasing one another in the garden or playing ball on the hastily mowed lawn.

'I've got something I have to do,' Finn told her. 'Come with me.'

He took her hand and led her across the room to stand framed in the French doors so people both inside and out could hear what he had to say.

'Ladies and gentlemen, I would like to thank you all for coming here today, and we look forward to seeing you all again when the restaurant finally opens.

I would also like to make an announcement. Not only are we celebrating the imminent opening of our new restaurant, but I would also like to make public my engagement to Hope Brown.' Smiling at the look of embarrassment on Hope's face, he fished in his pocket. 'Hope doesn't know anything about this, but I do have a ring to give her. It may not be a great big diamond, but I think she'll like it because belonged to my grandmother. I managed to save it from the things of hers I was forced to sell. As you all probably know, Hope was engaged to someone else before I came into her life, but as she was prepared to exchange a millionaire for a lowly chef, I know she must love me.'

Once the laughter and applause had died down, he drew her into his arms and slid a beautiful sapphire and diamond ring on to her finger.

'I love you, Hope Brown,' he declared.

A great cheer went up as he kissed her, and when the noise quietened a little Travis moved towards them and held up his hand for silence.

'I bought several pieces of furniture at the sale,' he said, 'but they belong here, in this house, so I would like to give them back to you both as an engagement present.'

Someone else called out, 'I bought the chandelier, Mr Masters, and that's going to be your wedding present — so don't wait too long to get married.'

This was followed by several more promises of furniture, mirrors and pictures that had been taken from the house and Hope felt tears in her eyes. Still happily snug in Finn's arms, she looked for Todd, but he had already left with his new girlfriend.

'Do I still get my third wish?' she asked.

Finn shook his head. 'You've already had all your wishes. All you've got to come now is the 'happily ever after' bit.'

She smiled blissfully as he bent to kiss her. 'Ah well. I suppose that will just have to do, then.'

We do hope that you have enjoyed reading this large print book.

Did you know that all of our titles are available for purchase?

We publish a wide range of high quality large print books including:
Romances, Mysteries, Classics
General Fiction
Non Fiction and Westerns

Special interest titles available in large print are:
The Little Oxford Dictionary
Music Book, Song Book
Hymn Book, Service Book

Also available from us courtesy of Oxford University Press:
Young Readers' Dictionary
(large print edition)
Young Readers' Thesaurus
(large print edition)

For further information or a free brochure, please contact us at:
Ulverscroft Large Print Books Ltd.,
The Green, Bradgate Road, Anstey,
Leicester, LE7 7FU, England.
Tel: (00 44) **0116 236 4325**
Fax: (00 44) **0116 234 0205**